DRAGON PUNCHER ISLAND

BY JAMES KOCHALKA

Other books by James Kochalka

ISBN: 978-1-60309-085-8
1.Children's Books
2. Dragons
3. Graphic Novels

Dragon Puncher Island © 2011 James Kochalka. Published by Top Shelf Productions, PO Box 1282, Marietta, GA 30061-1282, USA. Publishers: Brett Warnock and Chris Staros. Top Shelf Productions® and the Top Shelf logo are registered trademarks of Top Shelf Productions, Inc. All Rights Reserved. No part of this publication may be reproduced without permission, except for small excerpts for purposes of review. Visit our online catalog at www.topshelfcomix.com. First Printing, September 2011. Printed in Singapore.

Background photos taken on Monhegan Island in Maine.

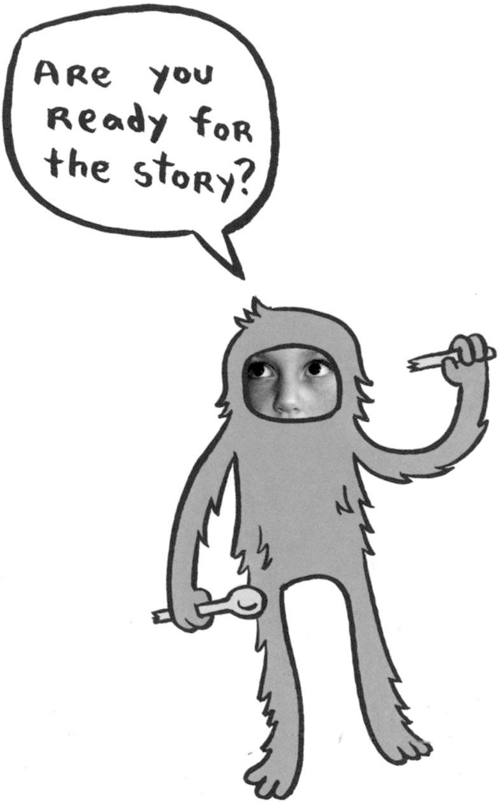
Are you ready for the story?

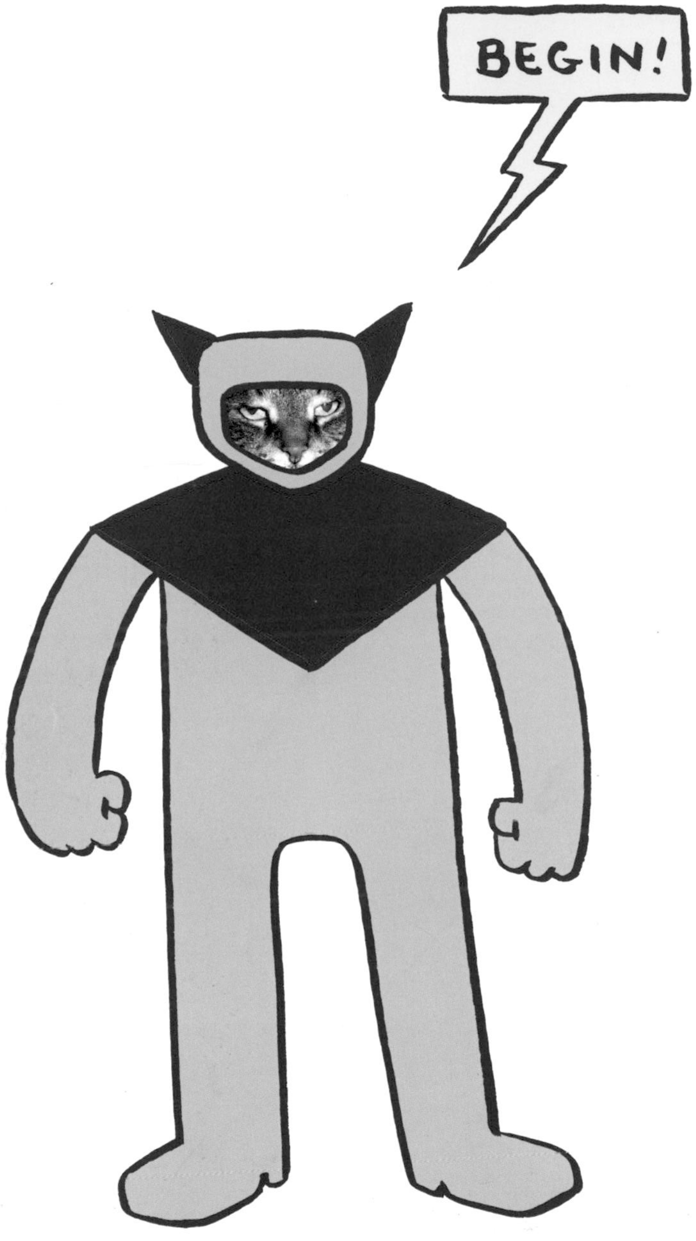
BEGIN!

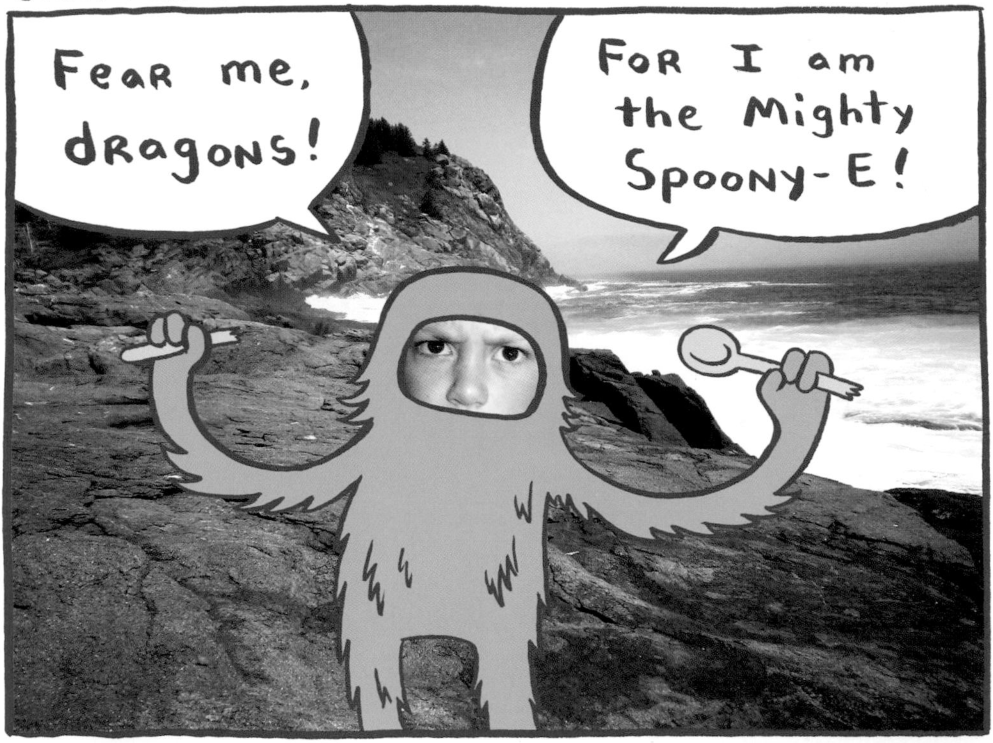
Fear me, dragons!
For I am the Mighty Spoony-E!

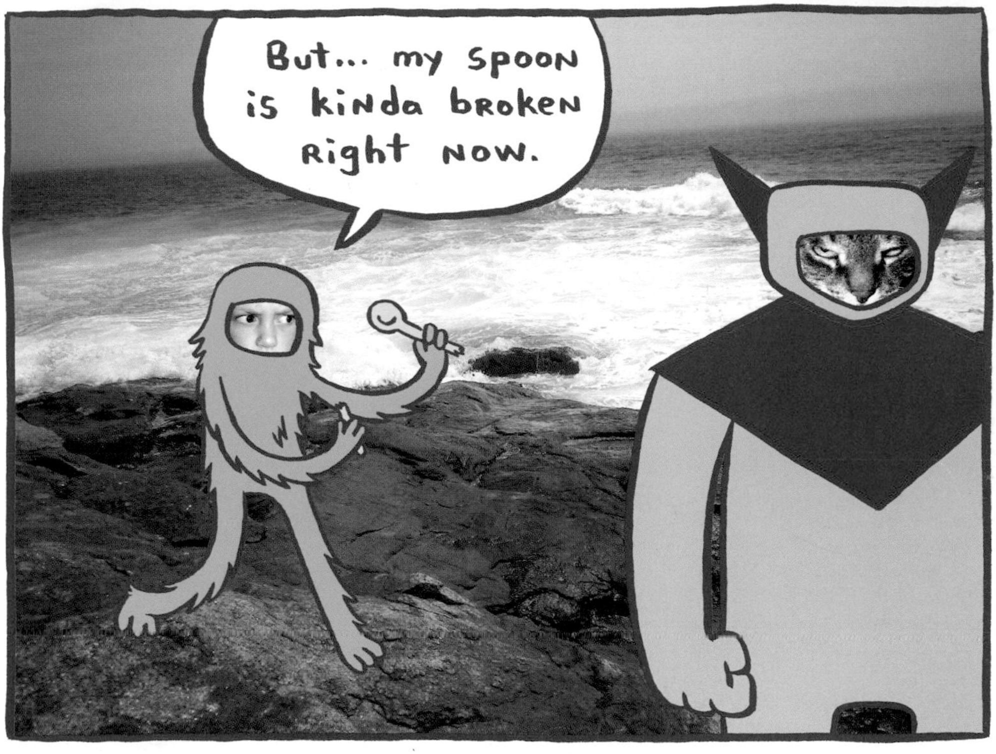
But... my spoon is kinda broken right now.

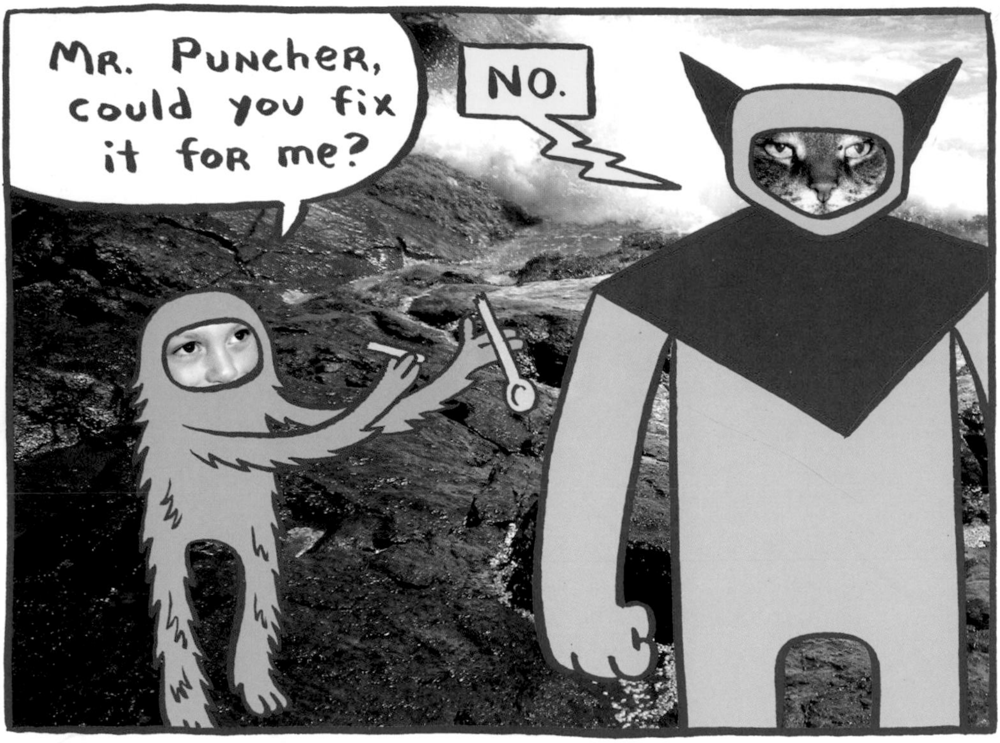
Mr. Puncher, could you fix it for me?
NO.

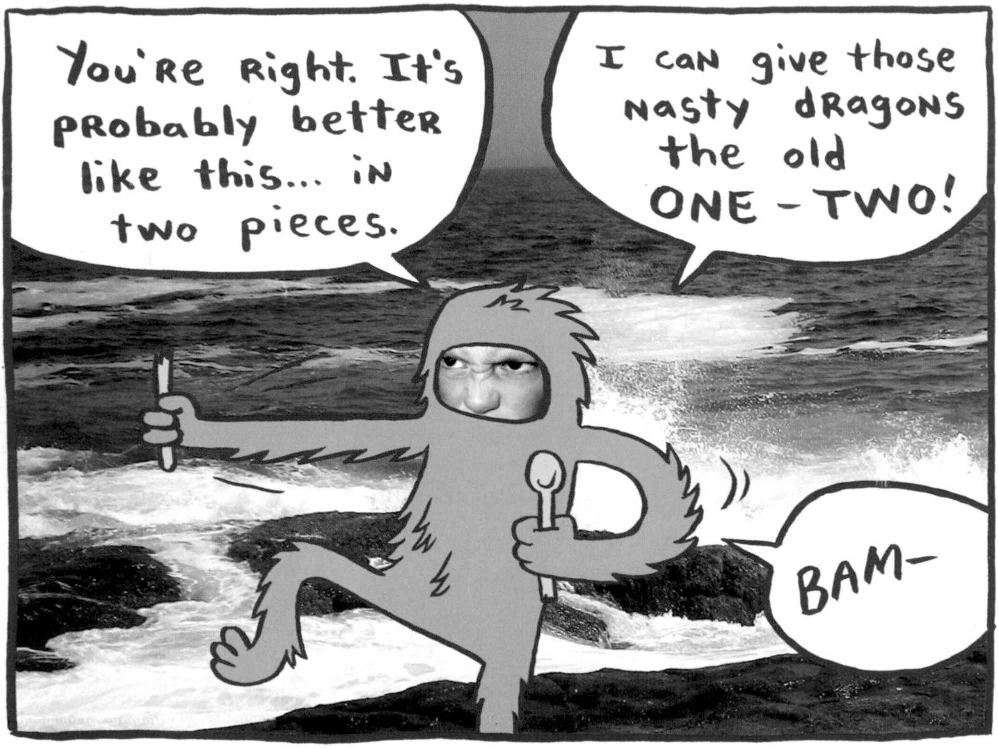
You're right. It's probably better like this... in two pieces.
I can give those nasty dragons the old ONE-TWO!
BAM-

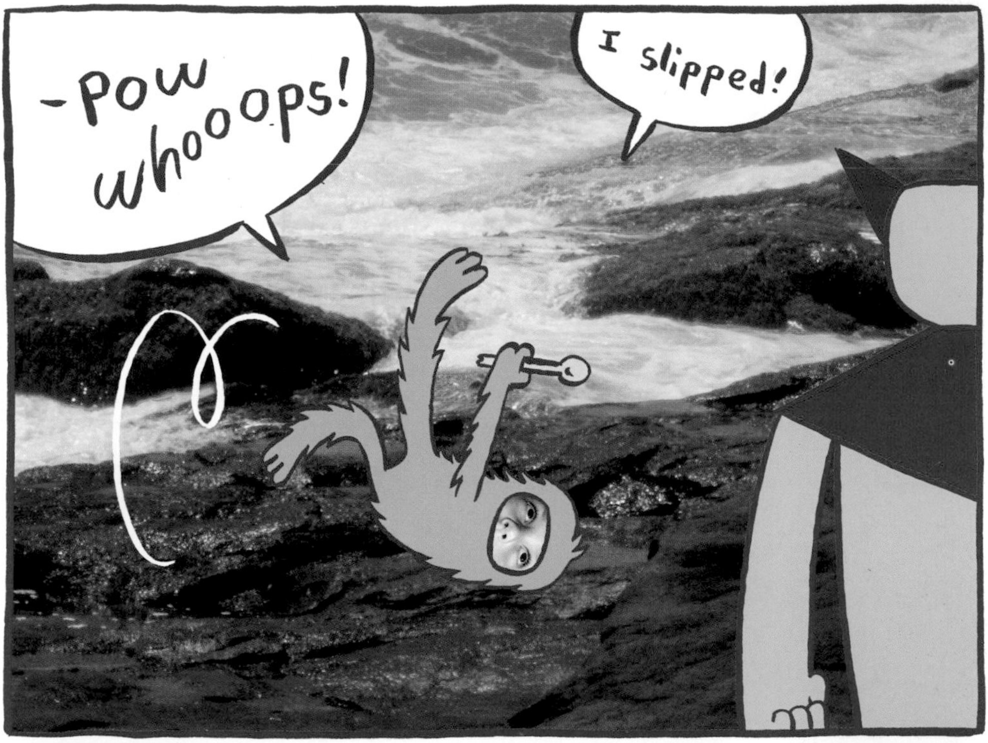
-Pow
whooops!
I slipped!

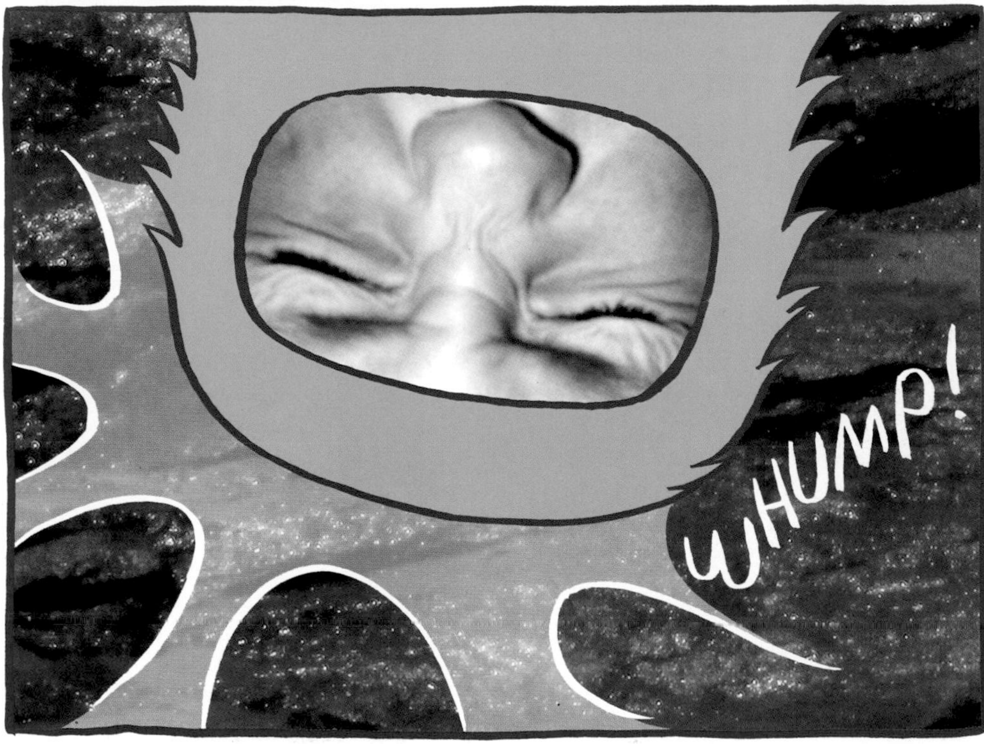
WHUMP!

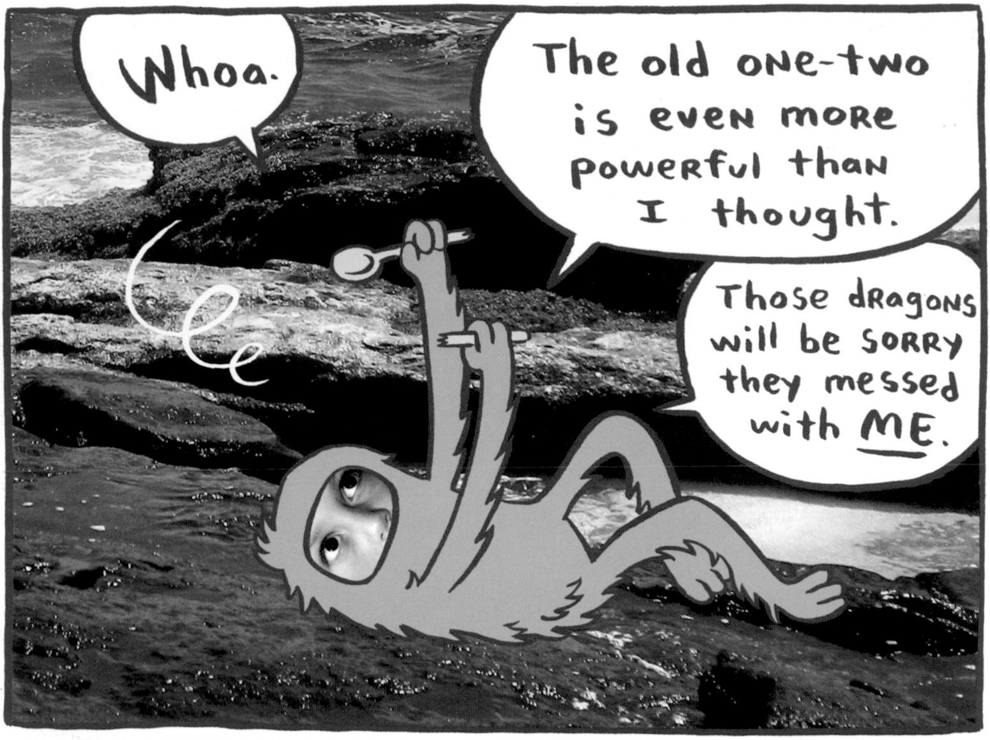
Whoa.
The old one-two is even more powerful than I thought.
Those dragons will be sorry they messed with ME.

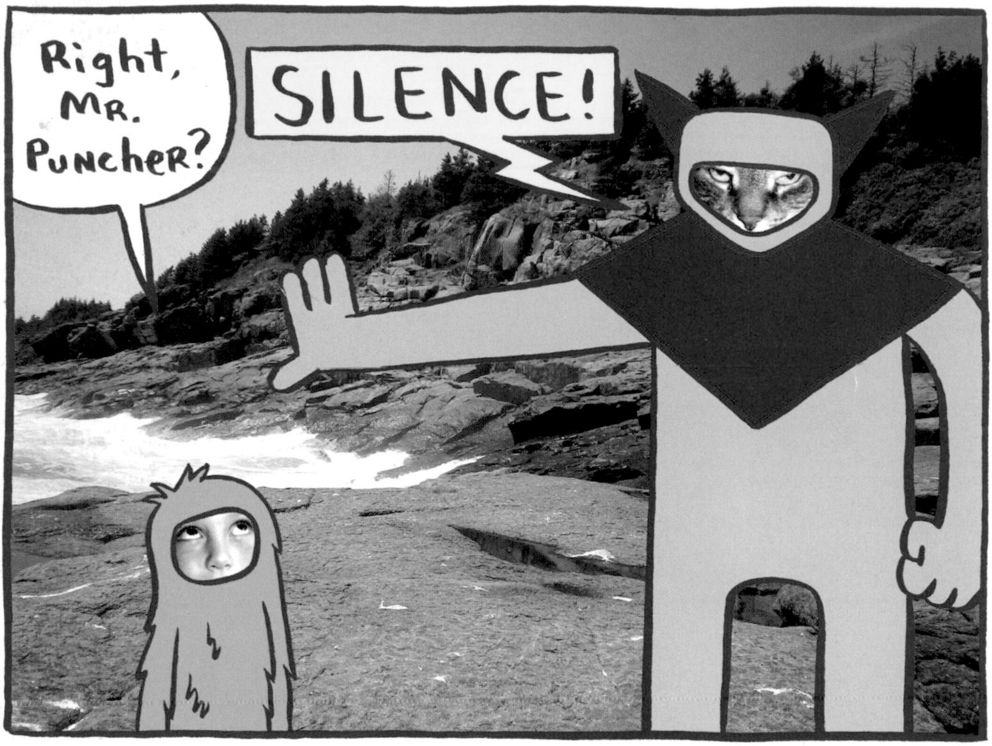
Right, Mr. Puncher?
SILENCE!

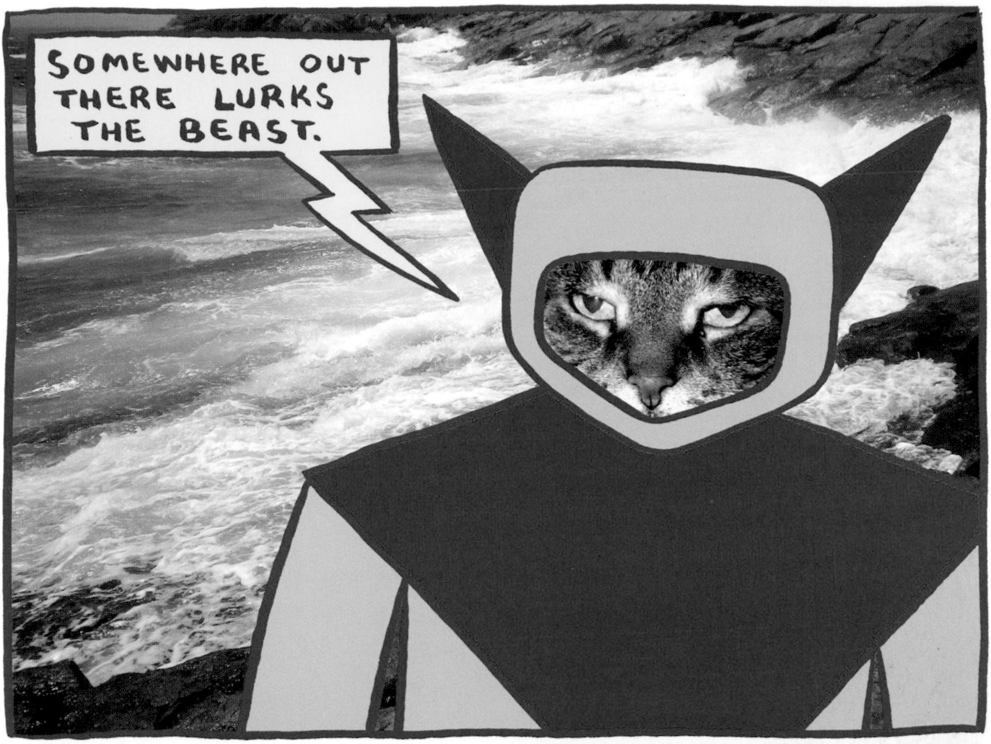
SOMEWHERE OUT THERE LURKS THE BEAST.

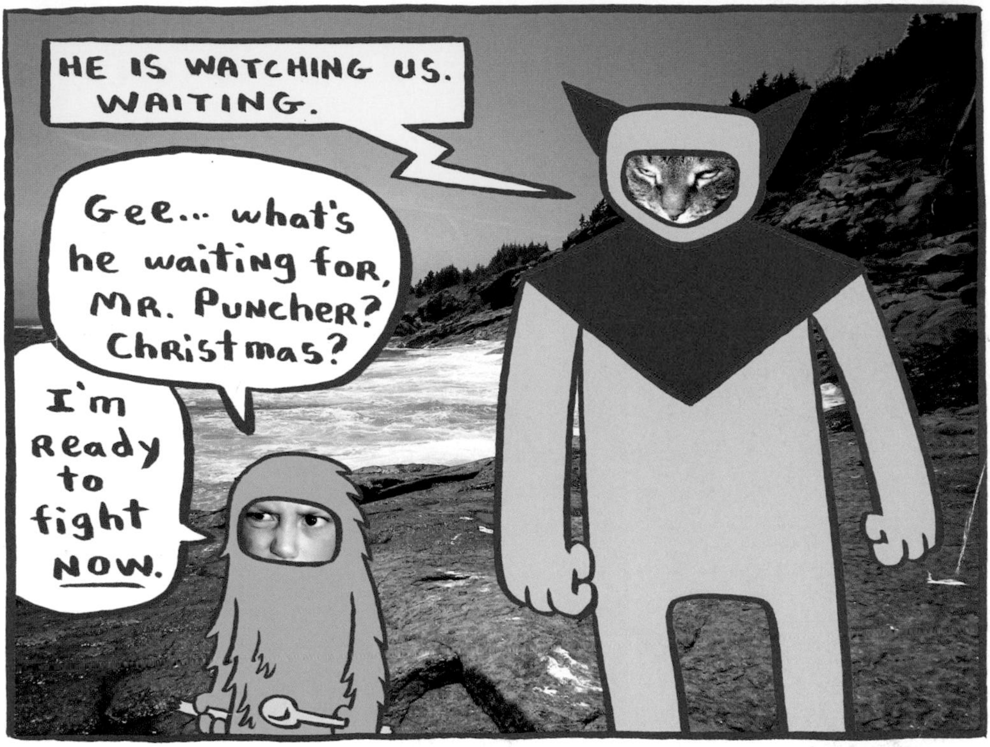
HE IS WATCHING US. WAITING.
Gee... what's he waiting for, Mr. Puncher? Christmas?
I'm ready to fight NOW.

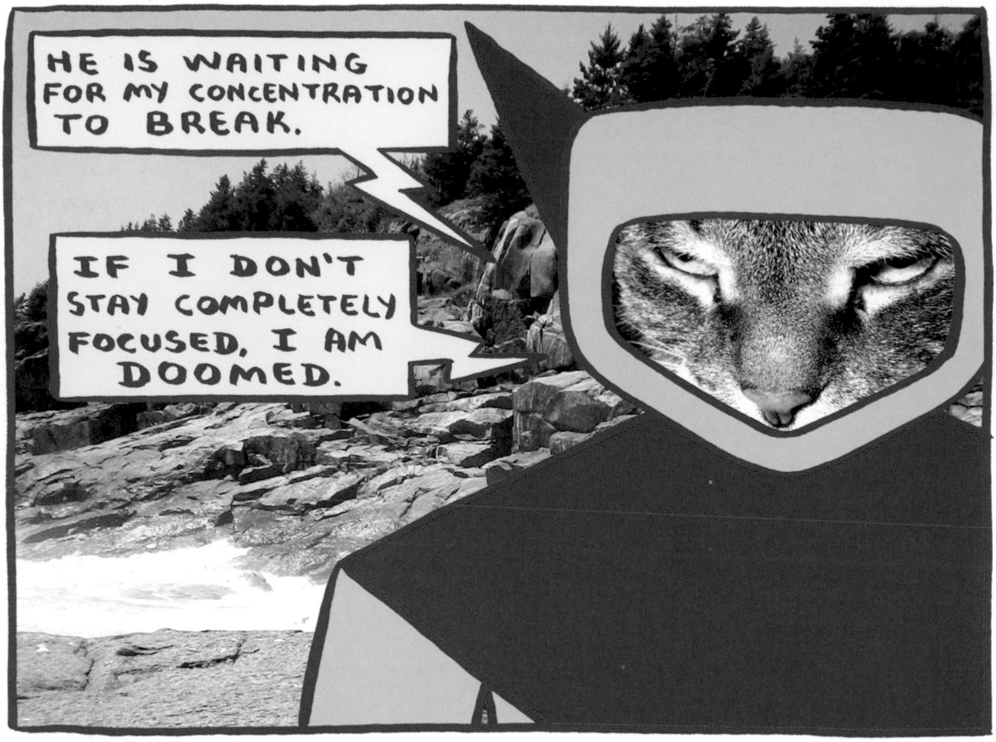
HE IS WAITING FOR MY CONCENTRATION TO BREAK.
IF I DON'T STAY COMPLETELY FOCUSED, I AM DOOMED.

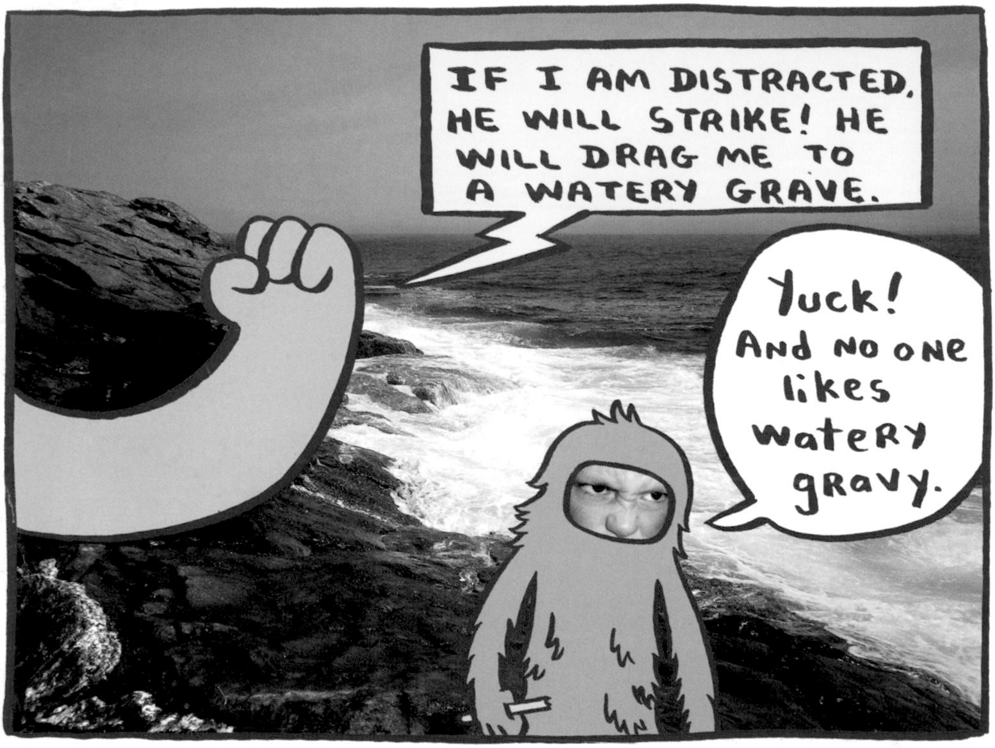
IF I AM DISTRACTED, HE WILL STRIKE! HE WILL DRAG ME TO A WATERY GRAVE.
Yuck! And no one likes watery gravy.

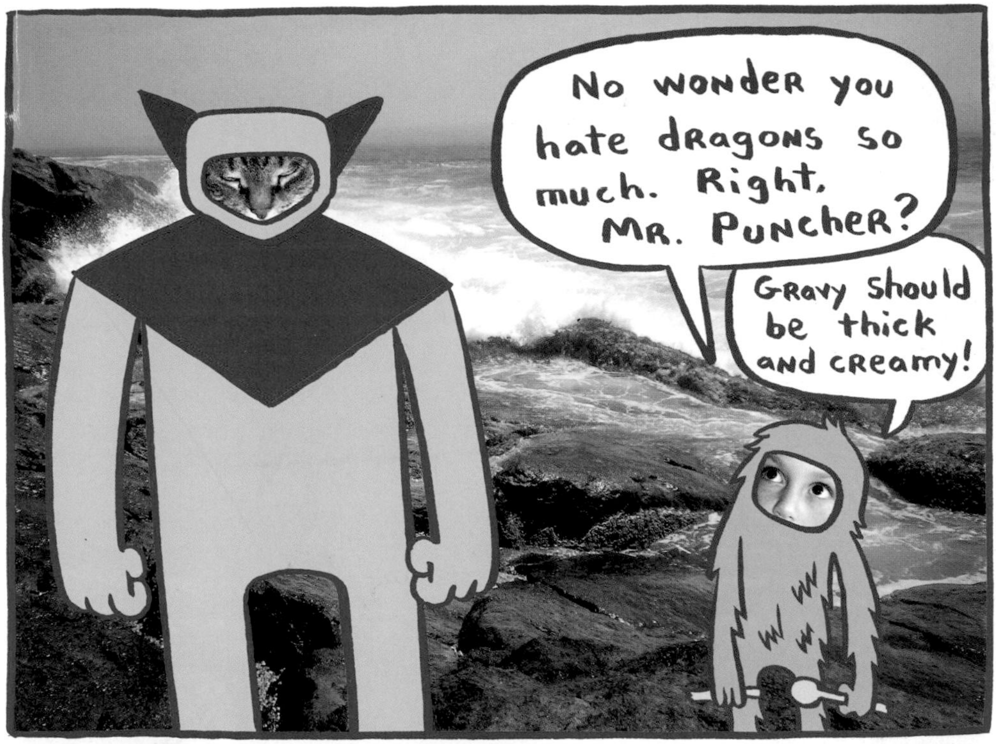
No wonder you hate dragons so much. Right, Mr. Puncher?
Gravy should be thick and creamy!

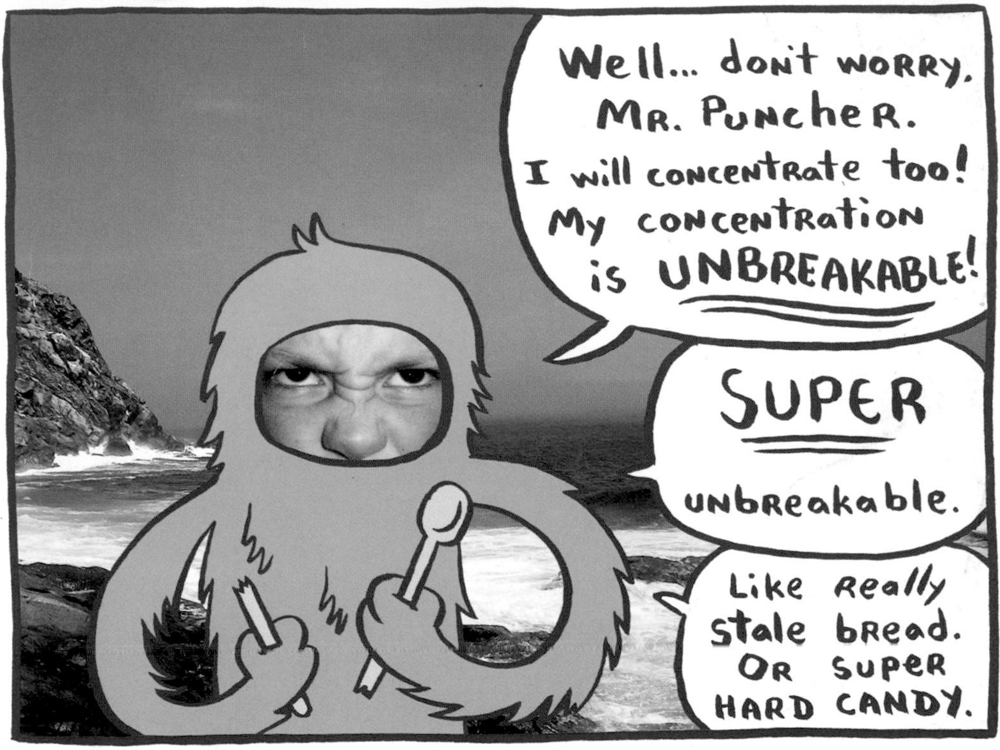
Well... don't worry, Mr. Puncher. I will concentrate too! My concentration is UNBREAKABLE!
SUPER unbreakable.
Like really stale bread. Or super hard candy.

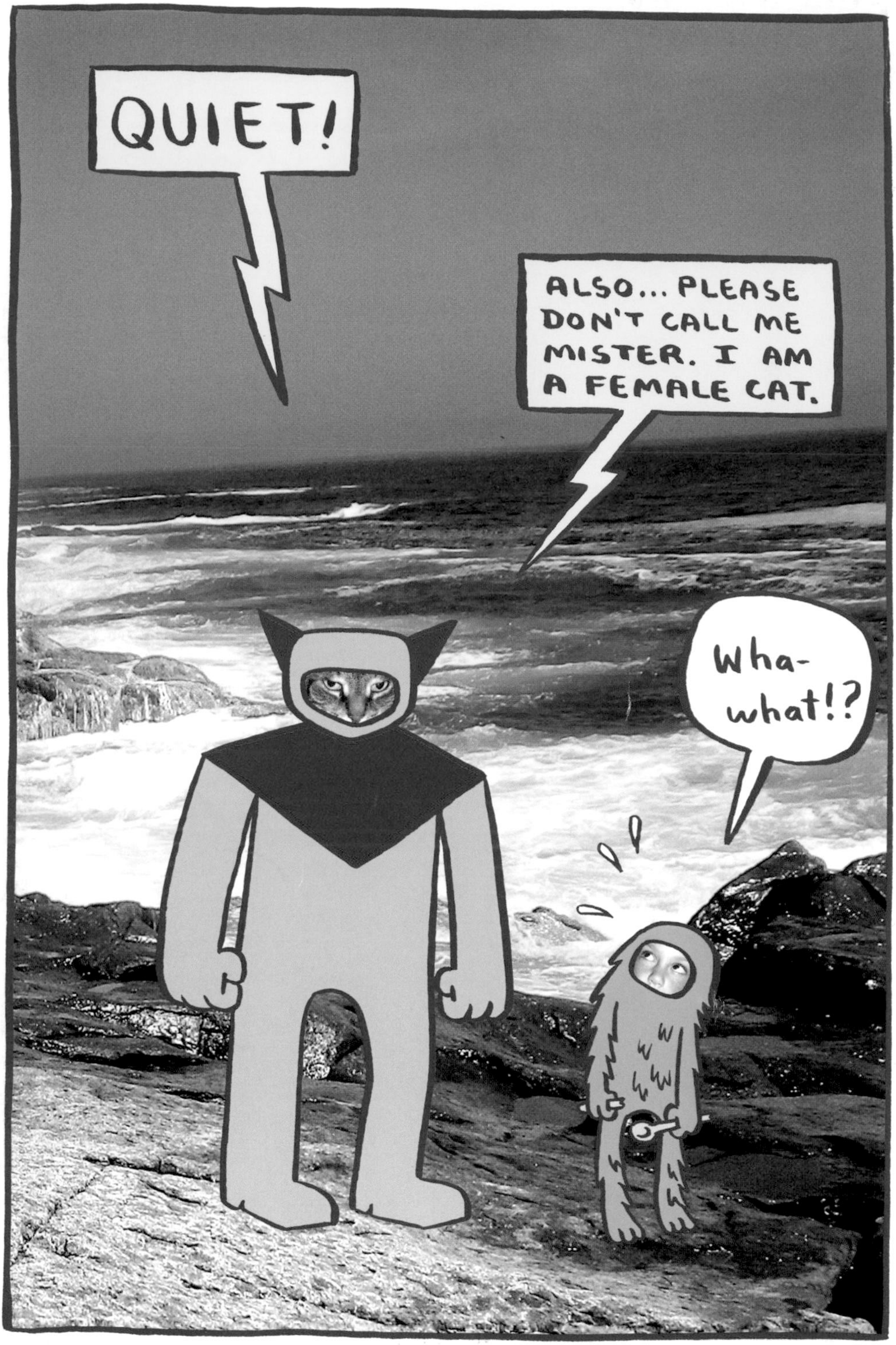
QUIET!
ALSO... PLEASE DON'T CALL ME MISTER. I AM A FEMALE CAT.
Wha-what!?

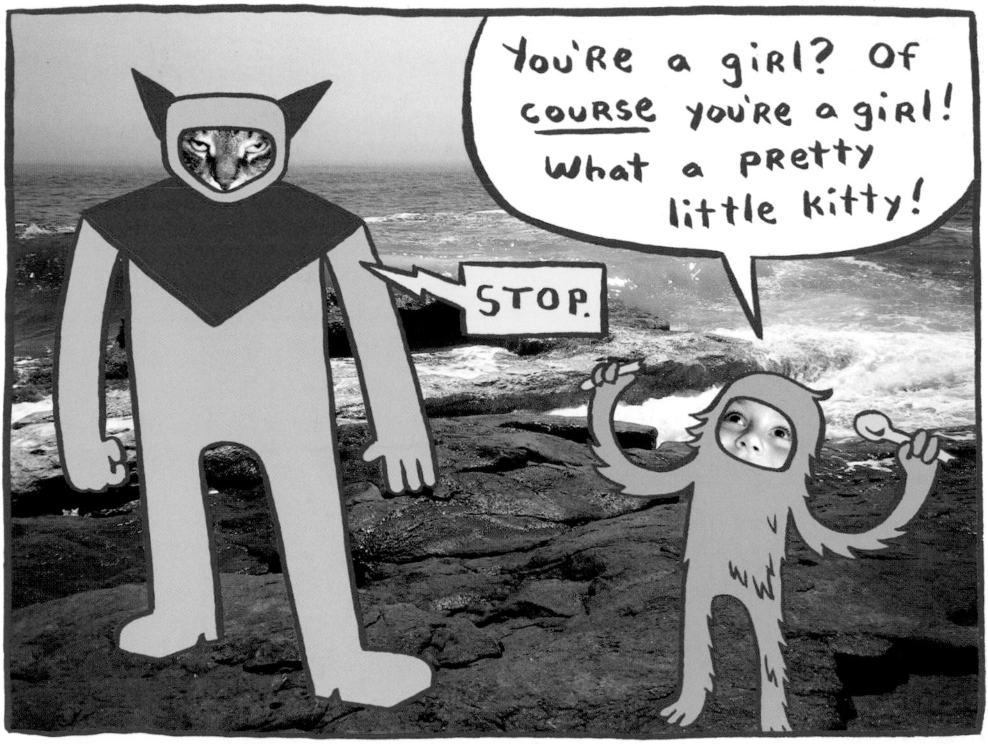
You're a girl? Of course you're a girl! What a pretty little kitty!
STOP.

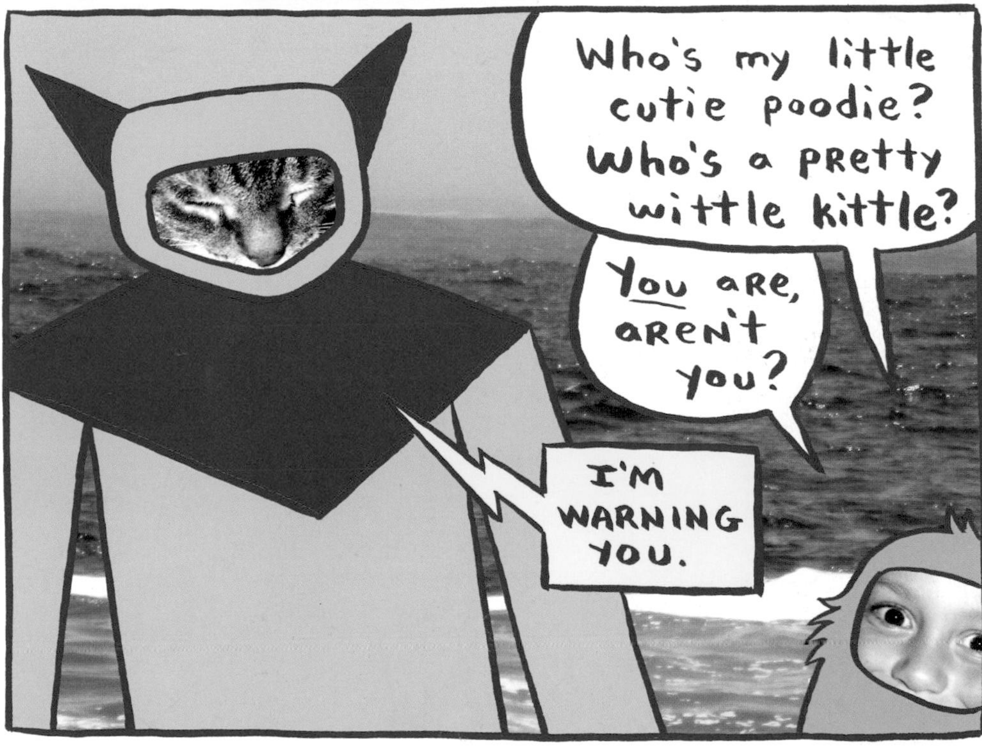
Who's my little cutie poodie? Who's a pretty wittle kittle?
You are, aren't you?
I'M WARNING YOU.

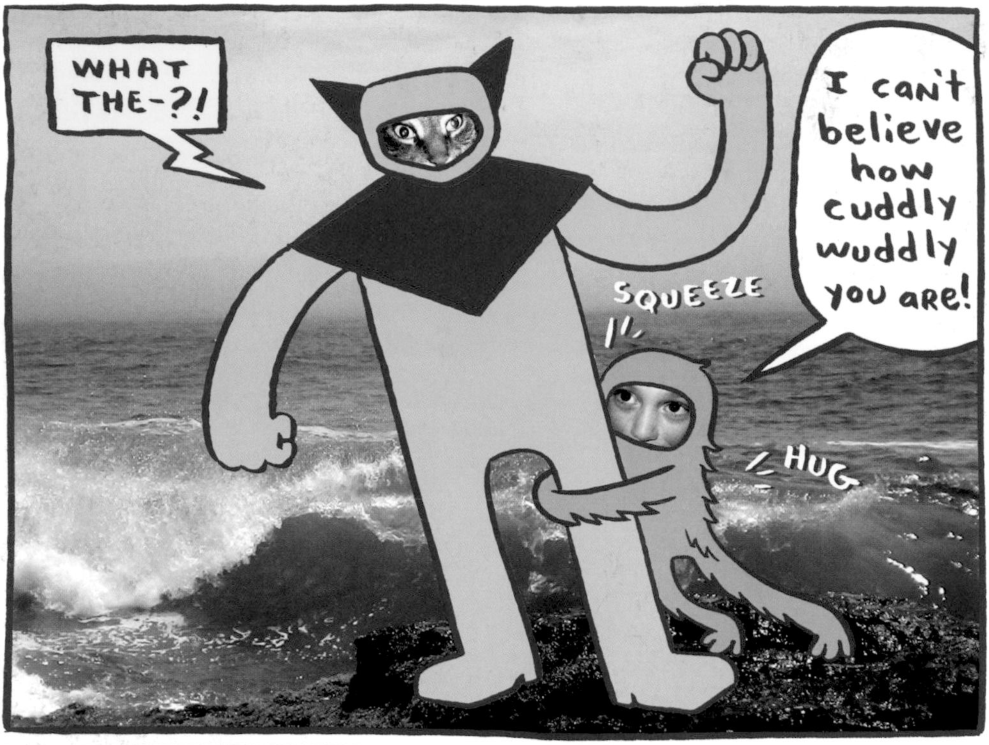
WHAT THE-?!
I can't believe how cuddly wuddly you are!
SQUEEZE
HUG

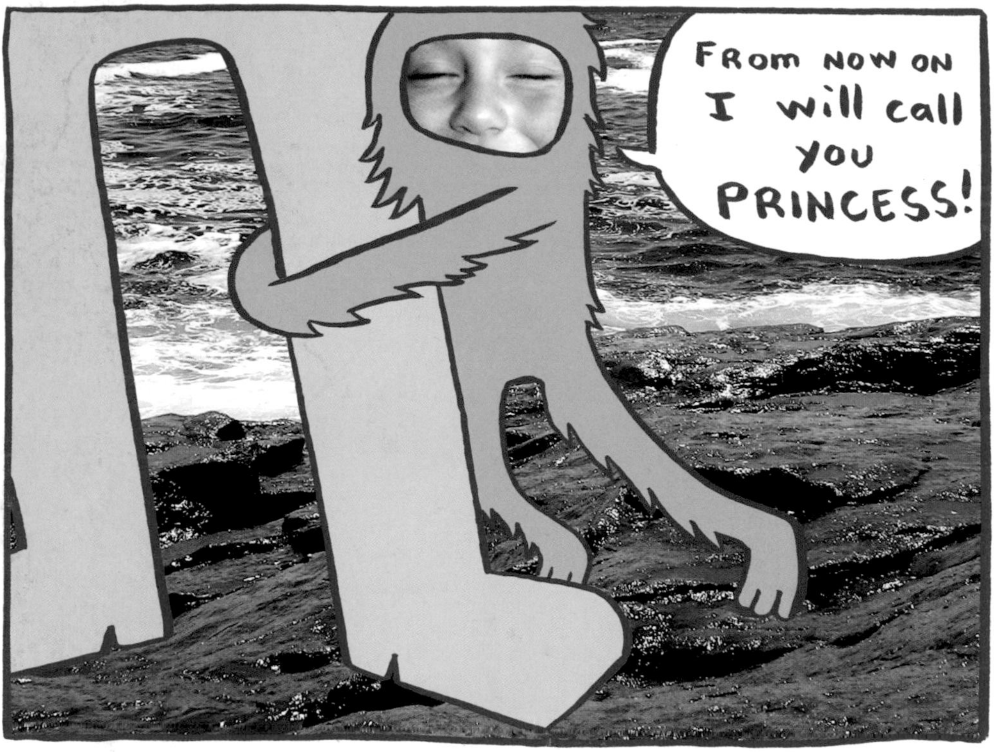
FROM NOW ON I will call you PRINCESS!

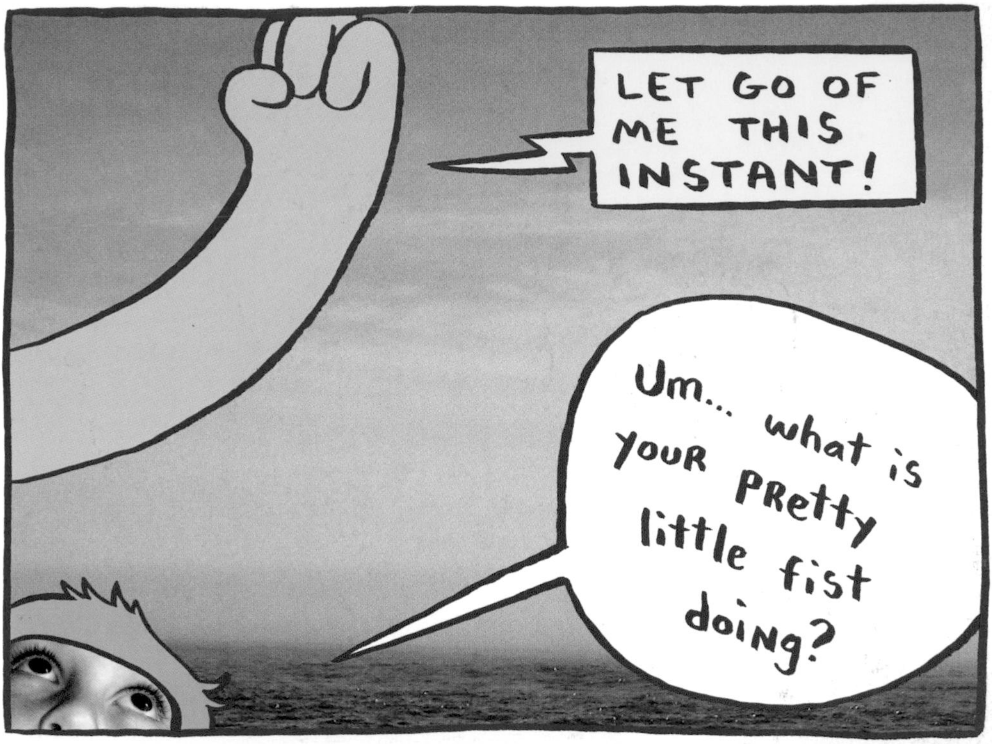
LET GO OF ME THIS INSTANT!
Um... what is your pretty little fist doing?

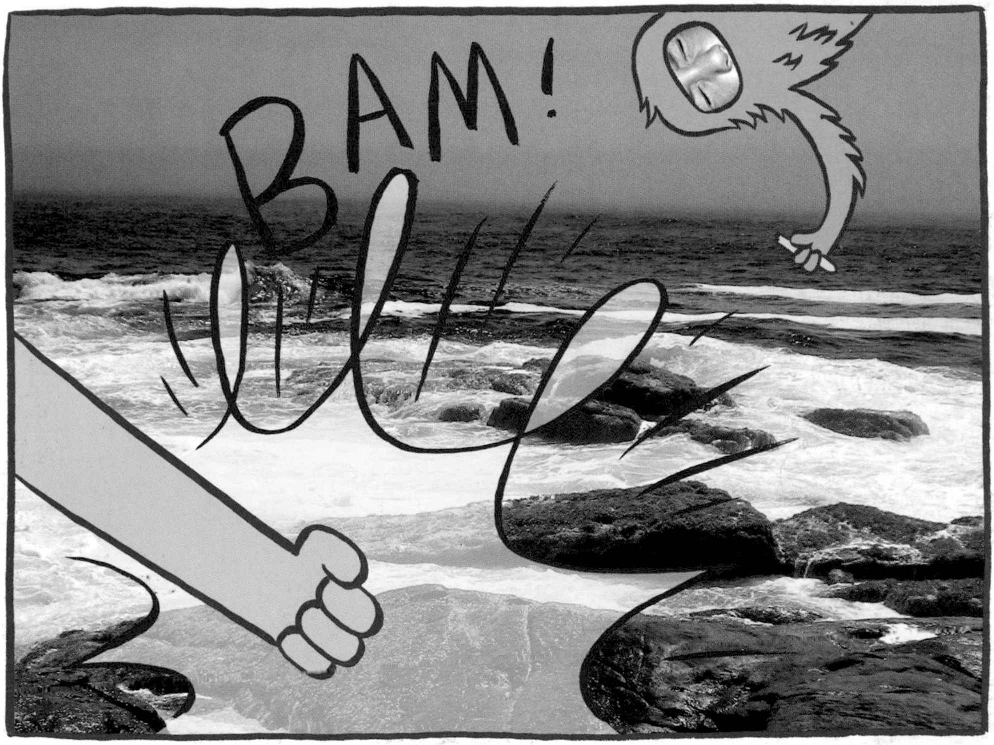
BAM!

I'm going to fall in the watery gravy and be swallowed up by the crazy gravy dragon!
I'm DOOMED!

CATCH!
I'm saved!

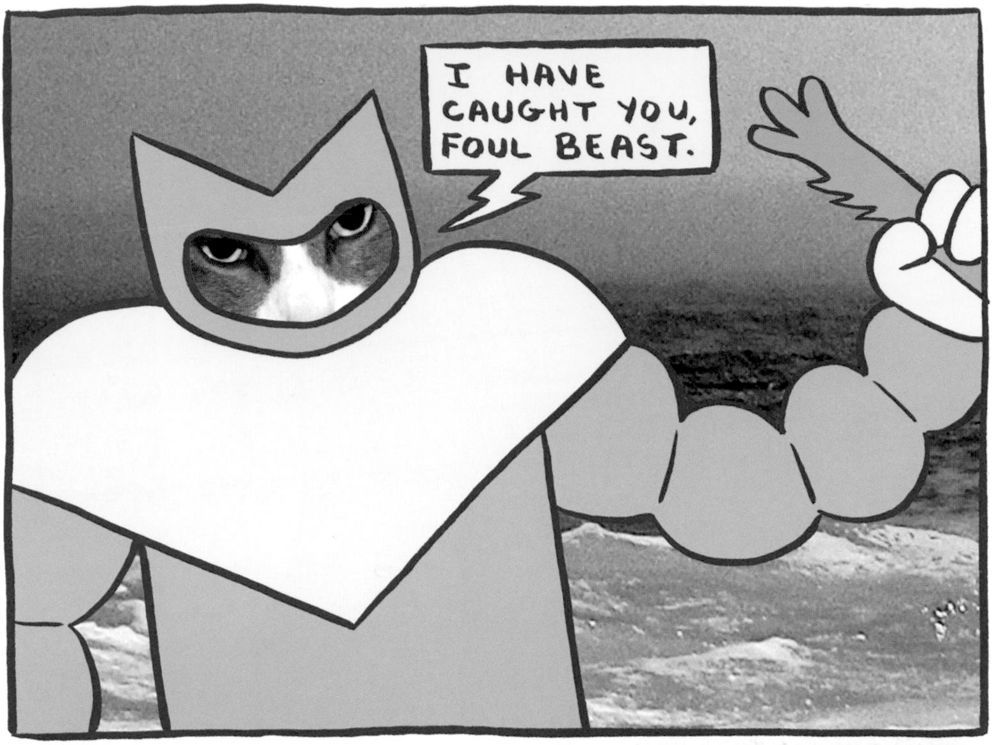

I HAVE CAUGHT YOU, FOUL BEAST.

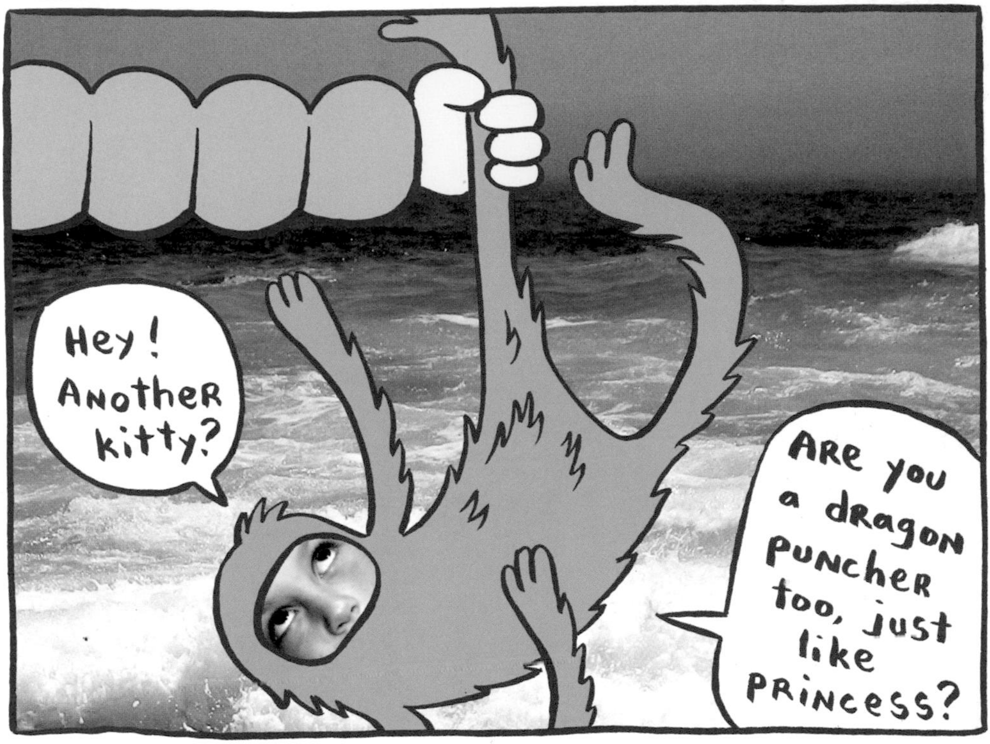

Hey! Another kitty?
Are you a dragon puncher too, just like Princess?

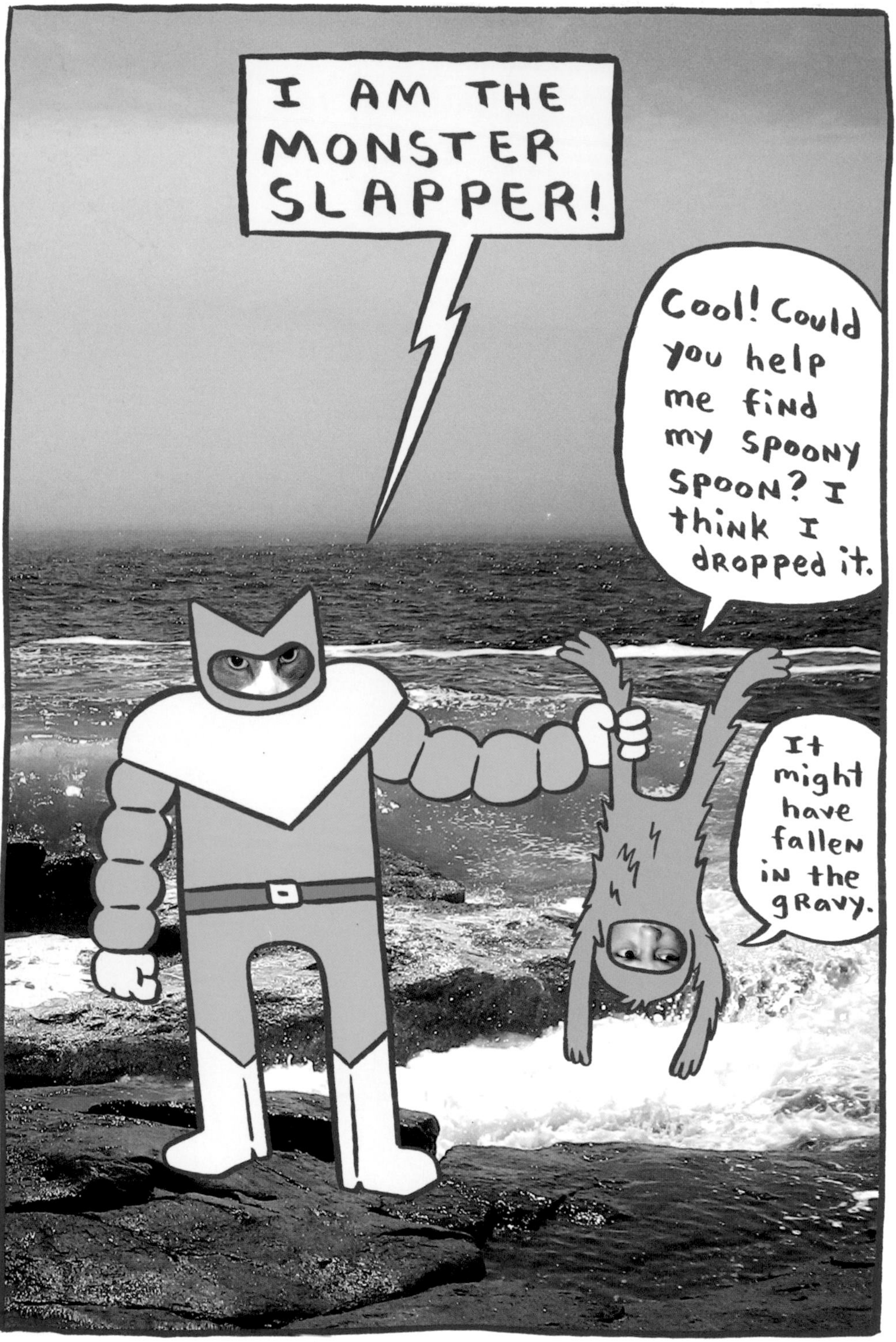
I AM THE MONSTER SLAPPER!
Cool! Could you help me find my spoony spoon? I think I dropped it.
It might have fallen in the gravy.

CHAPTER THREE

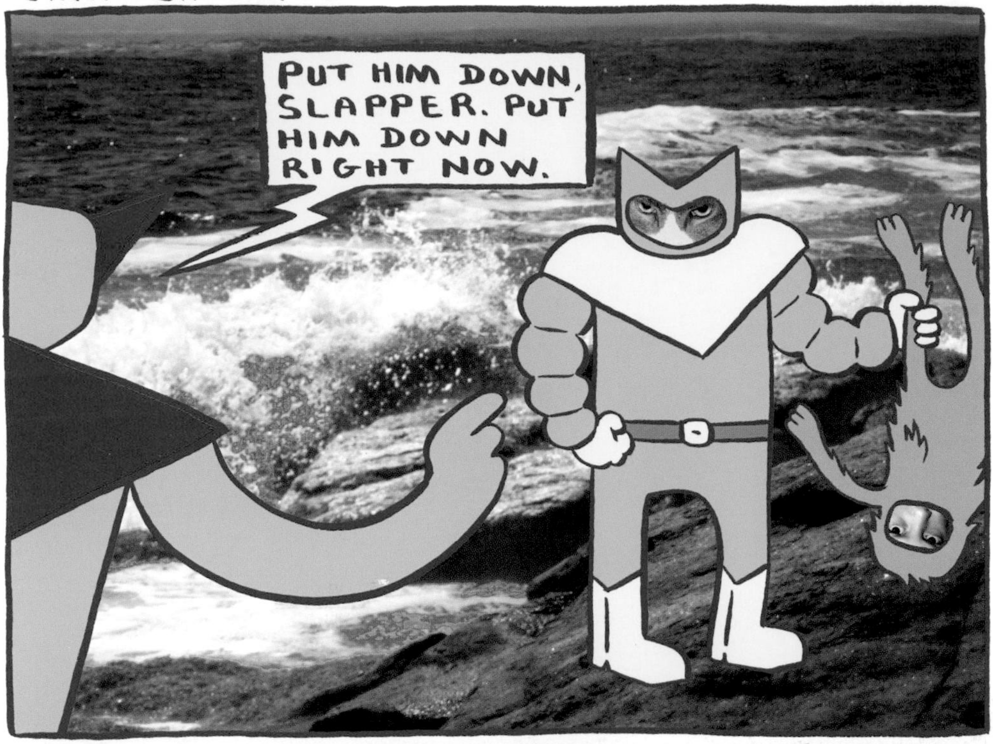
PUT HIM DOWN, SLAPPER. PUT HIM DOWN RIGHT NOW.

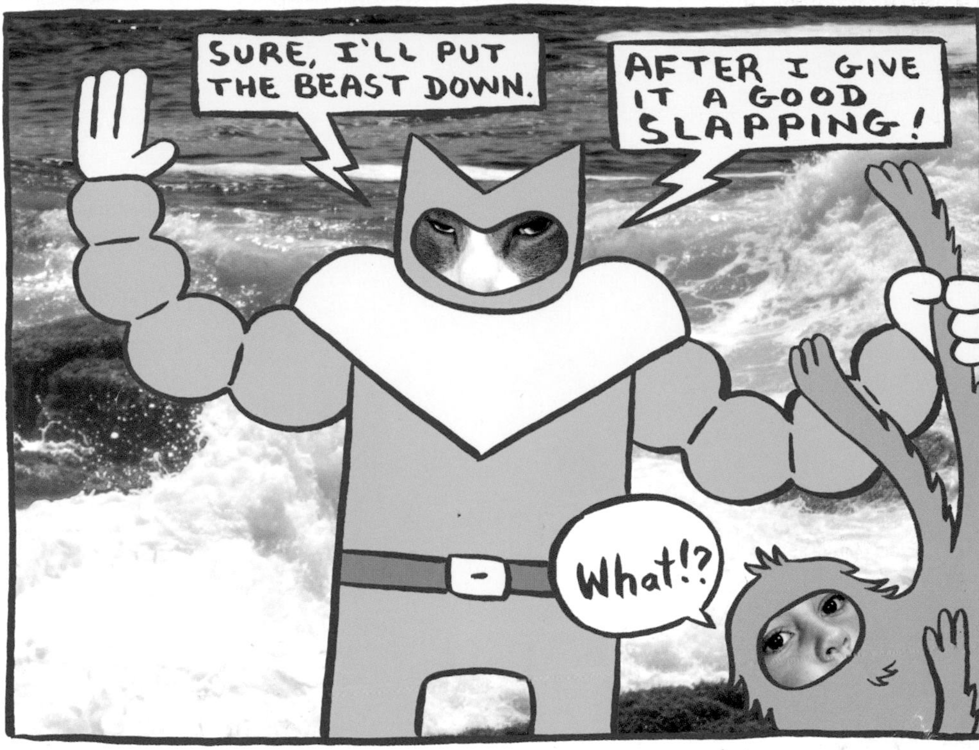
SURE, I'LL PUT THE BEAST DOWN.
AFTER I GIVE IT A GOOD SLAPPING!
What!?

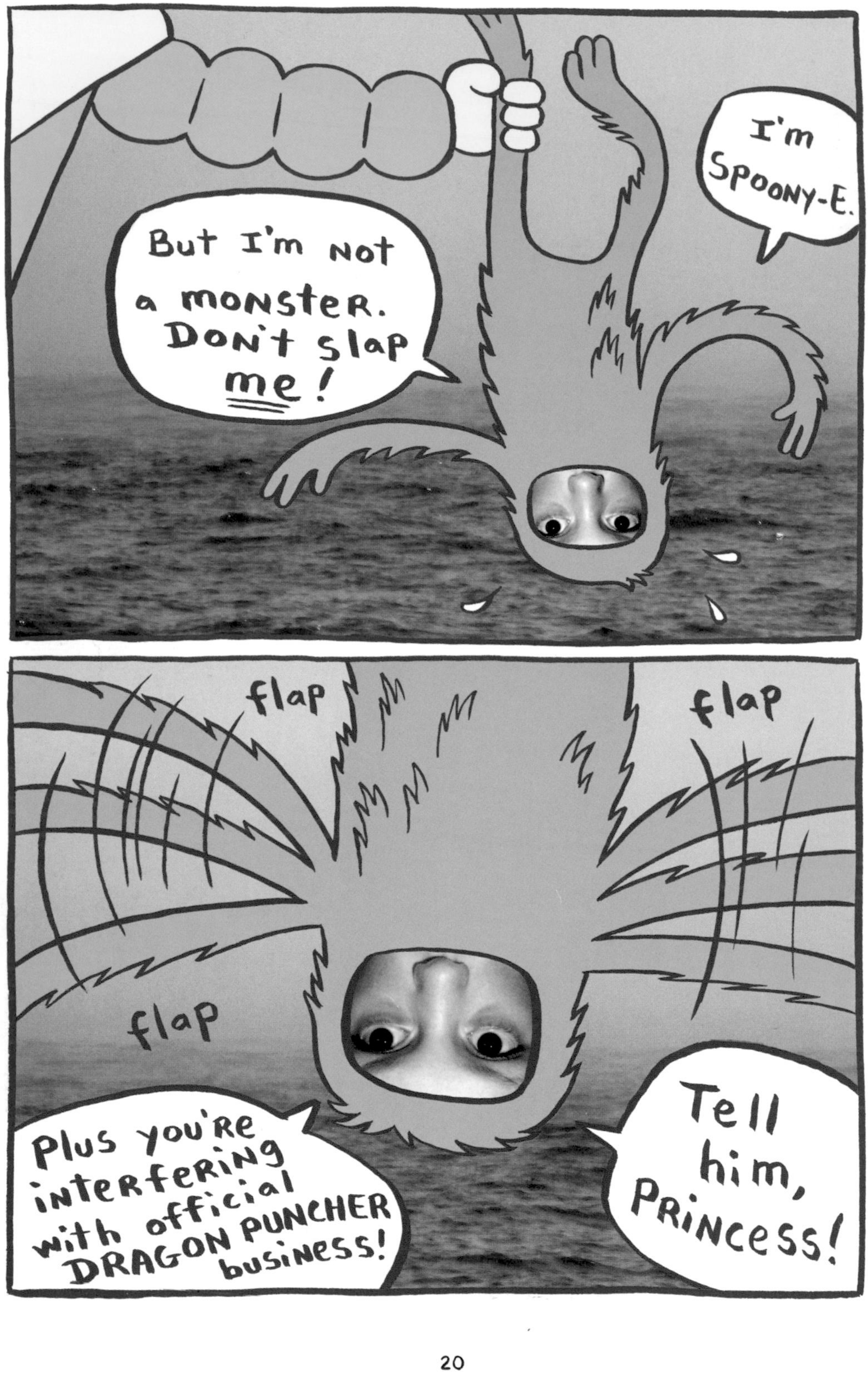
I'm Spoony-E.
But I'm not a monster. Don't slap me!
flap
flap
flap
Plus you're interfering with official DRAGON PUNCHER business!
Tell him, PRINCESS!

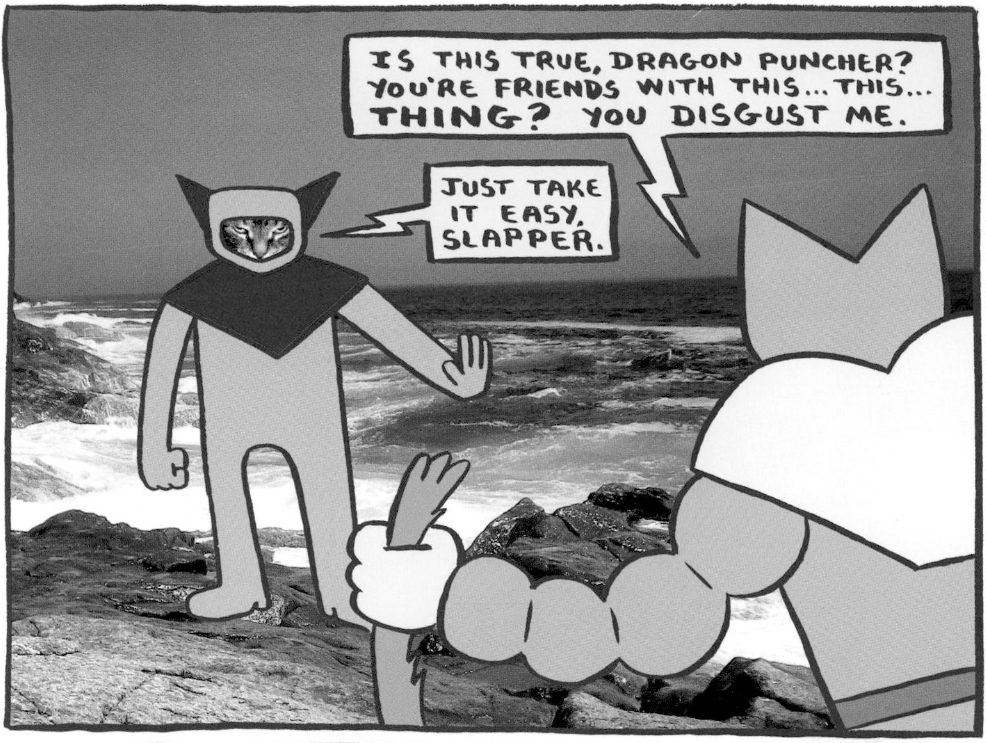
IS THIS TRUE, DRAGON PUNCHER? YOU'RE FRIENDS WITH THIS... THIS... THING? YOU DISGUST ME.
JUST TAKE IT EASY, SLAPPER.

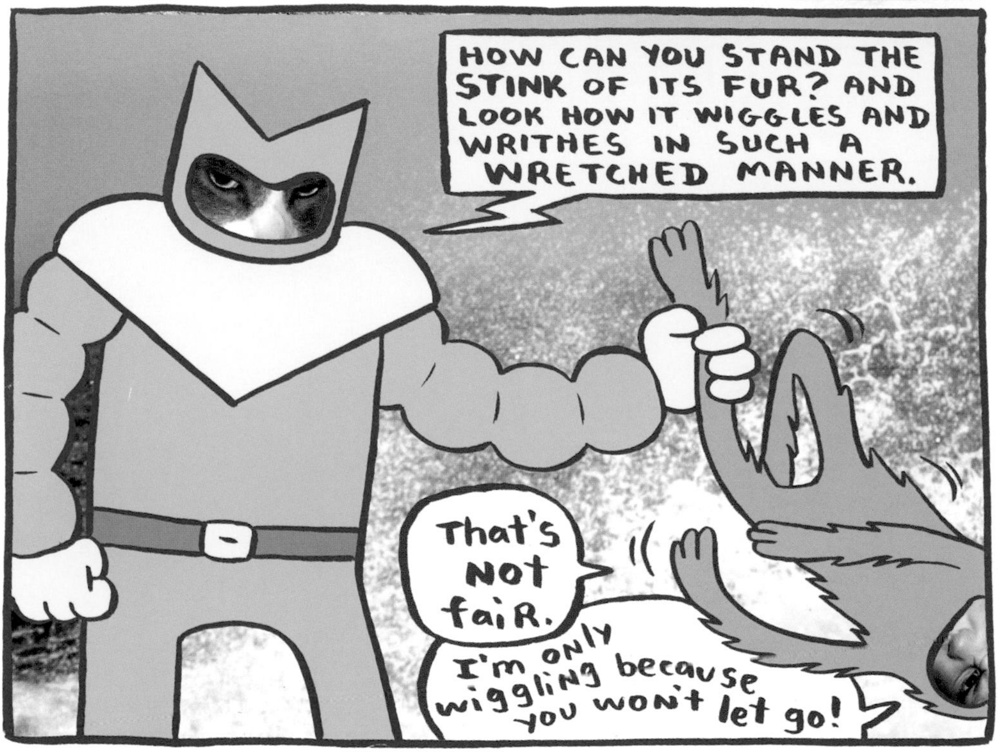
HOW CAN YOU STAND THE STINK OF ITS FUR? AND LOOK HOW IT WIGGLES AND WRITHES IN SUCH A WRETCHED MANNER.
That's NOT faiR.
I'm only wiggling because you won't let go!

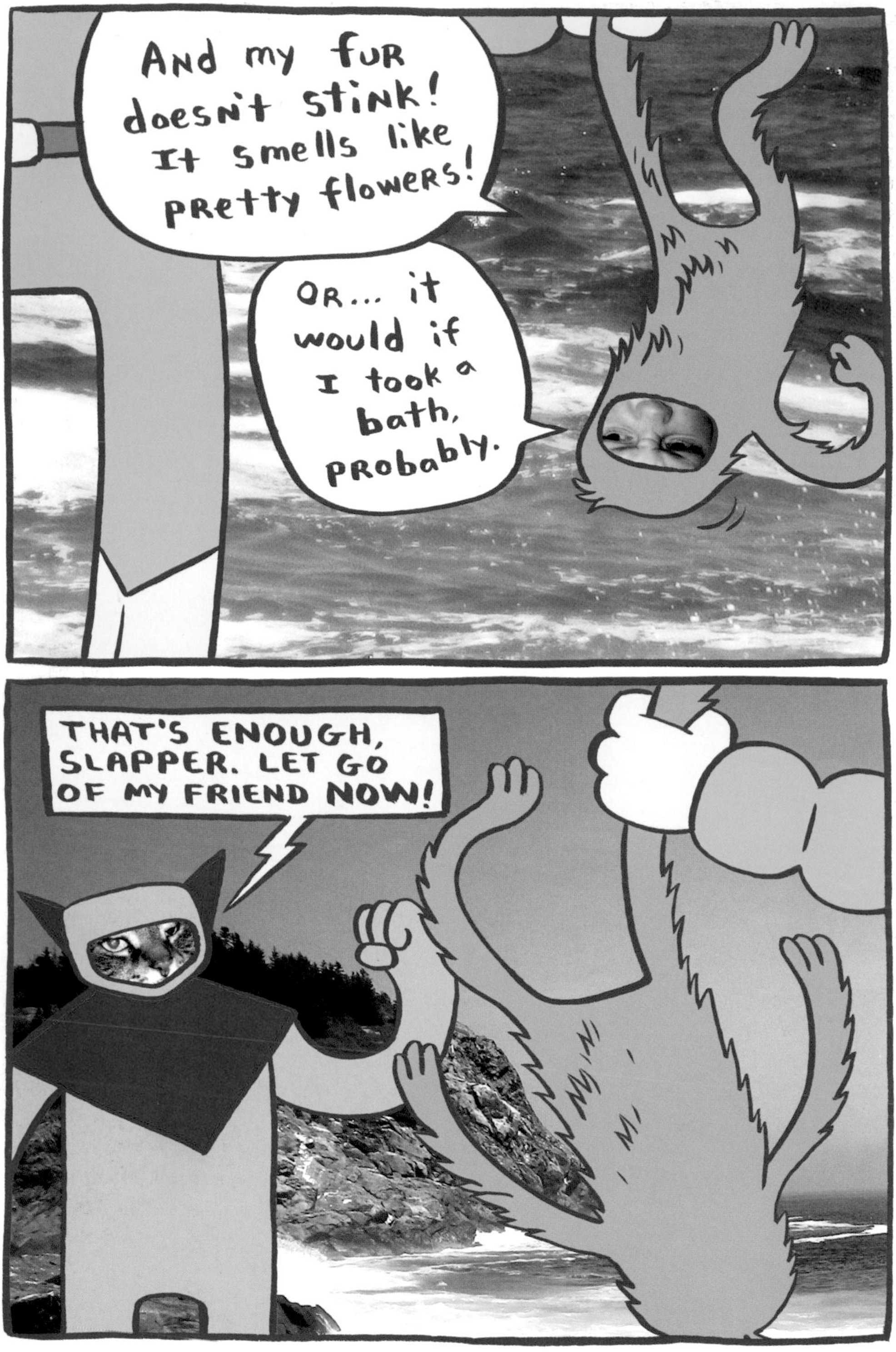
And my fur doesn't stink! It smells like pretty flowers!
Or... it would if I took a bath, probably.
THAT'S ENOUGH, SLAPPER. LET GO OF MY FRIEND NOW!

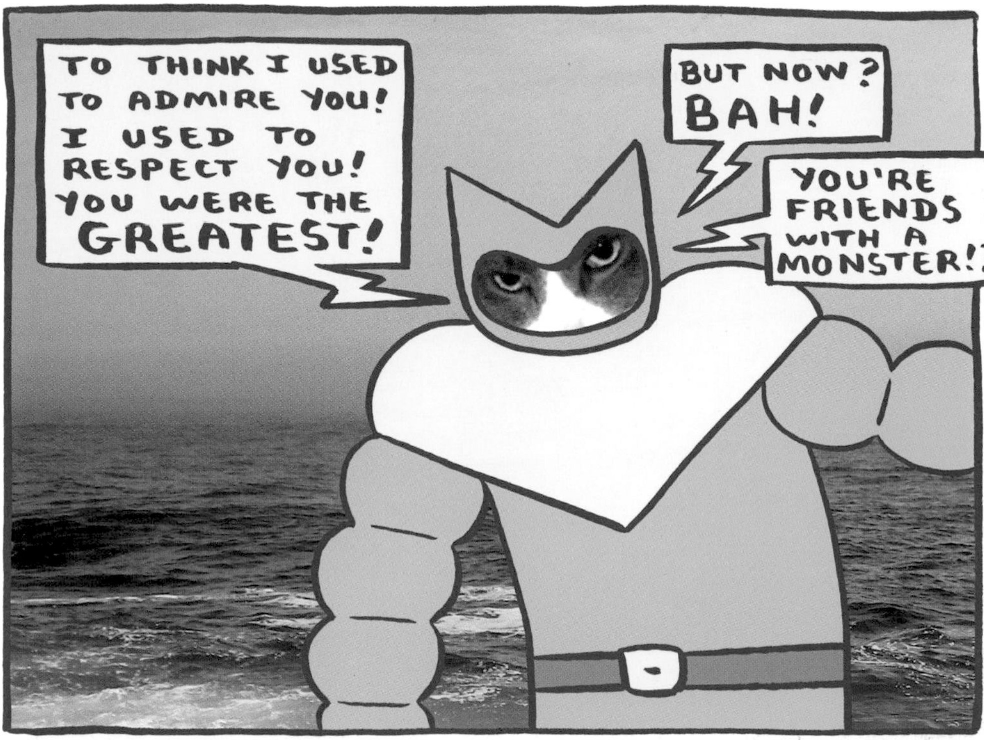
TO THINK I USED TO ADMIRE YOU! I USED TO RESPECT YOU! YOU WERE THE GREATEST!
BUT NOW? BAH!
YOU'RE FRIENDS WITH A MONSTER!?

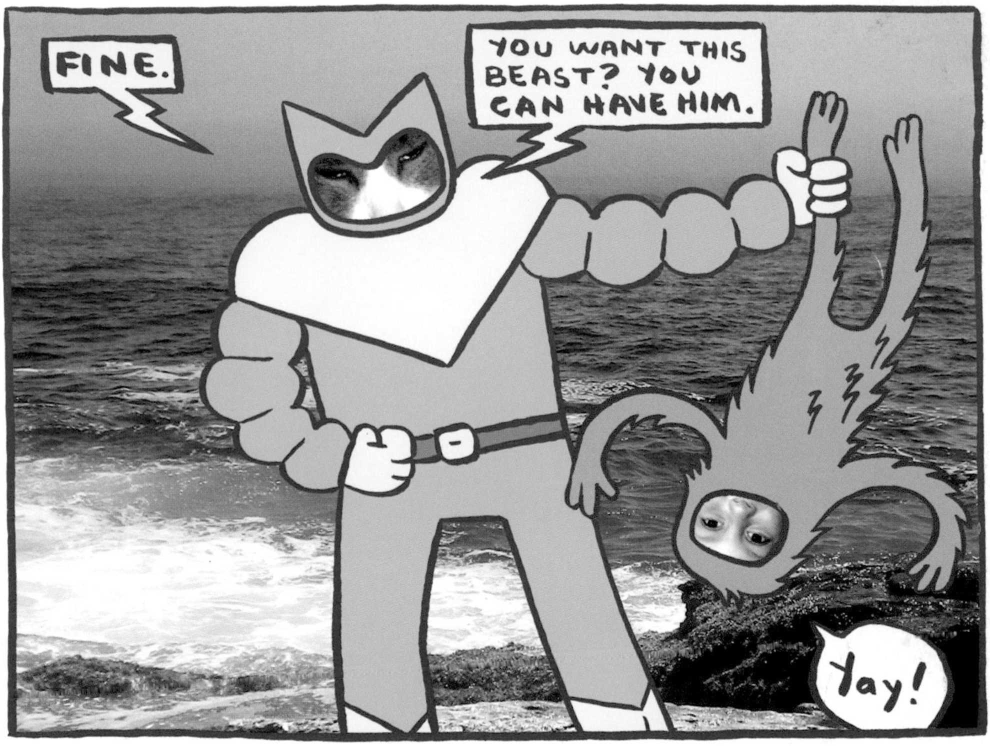
FINE.
YOU WANT THIS BEAST? YOU CAN HAVE HIM.
Yay!

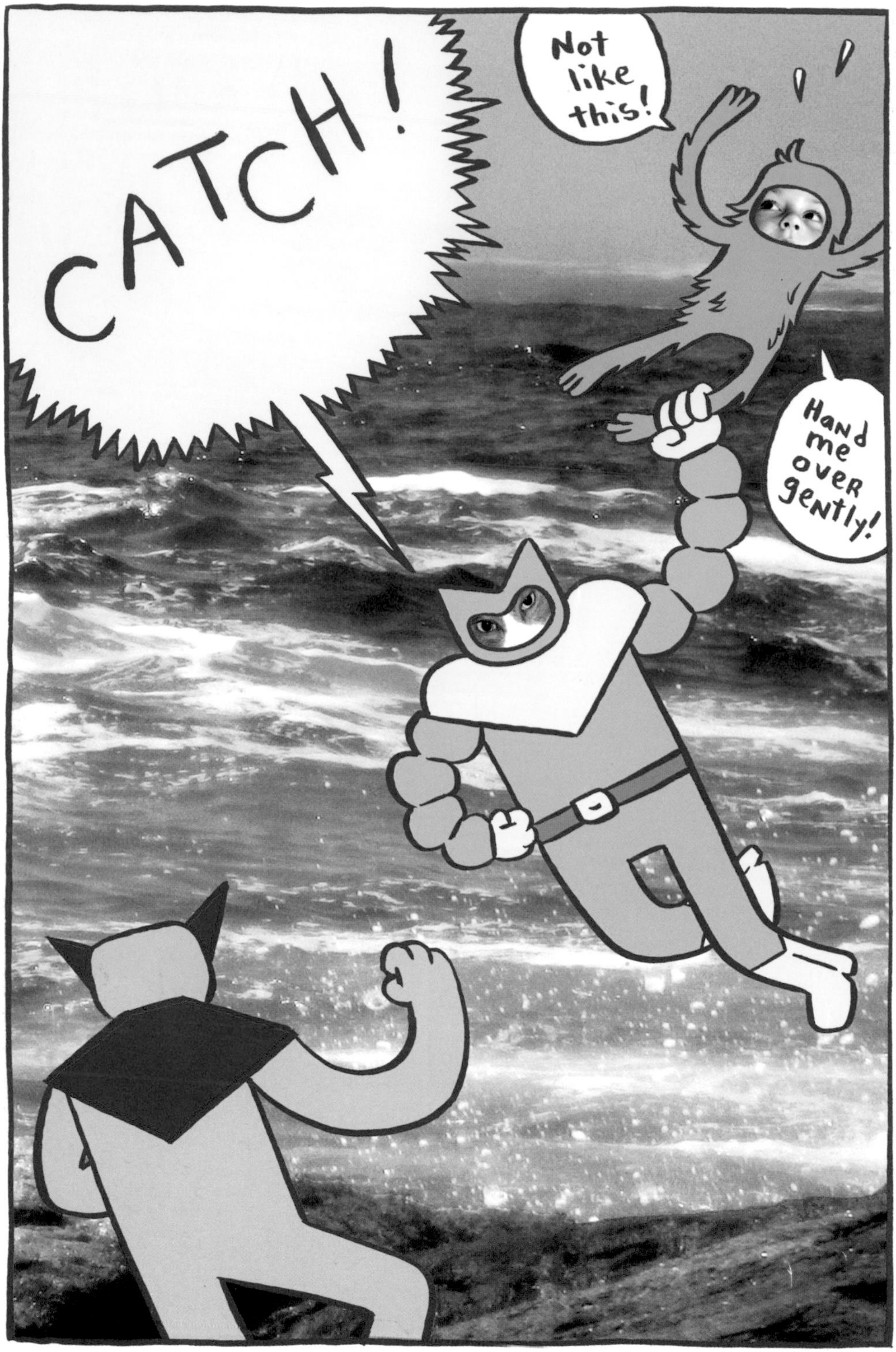
CATCH!
Not like this!
Hand me over gently!

CHAPTER FOUR:

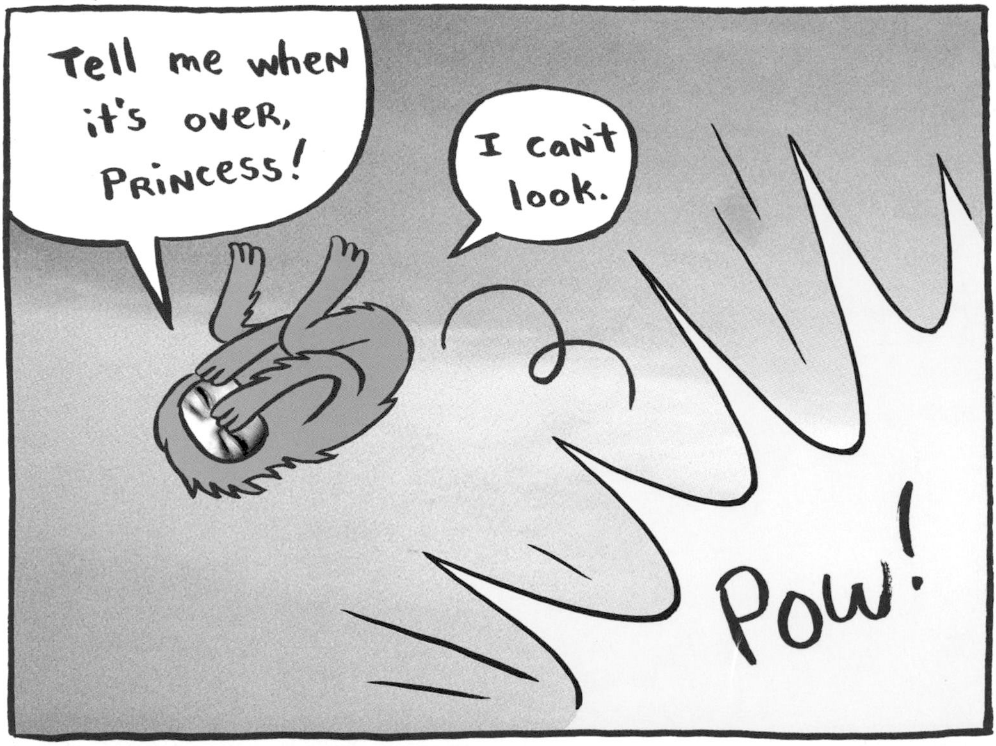
Tell me when it's over, Princess!
I can't look.
POW!

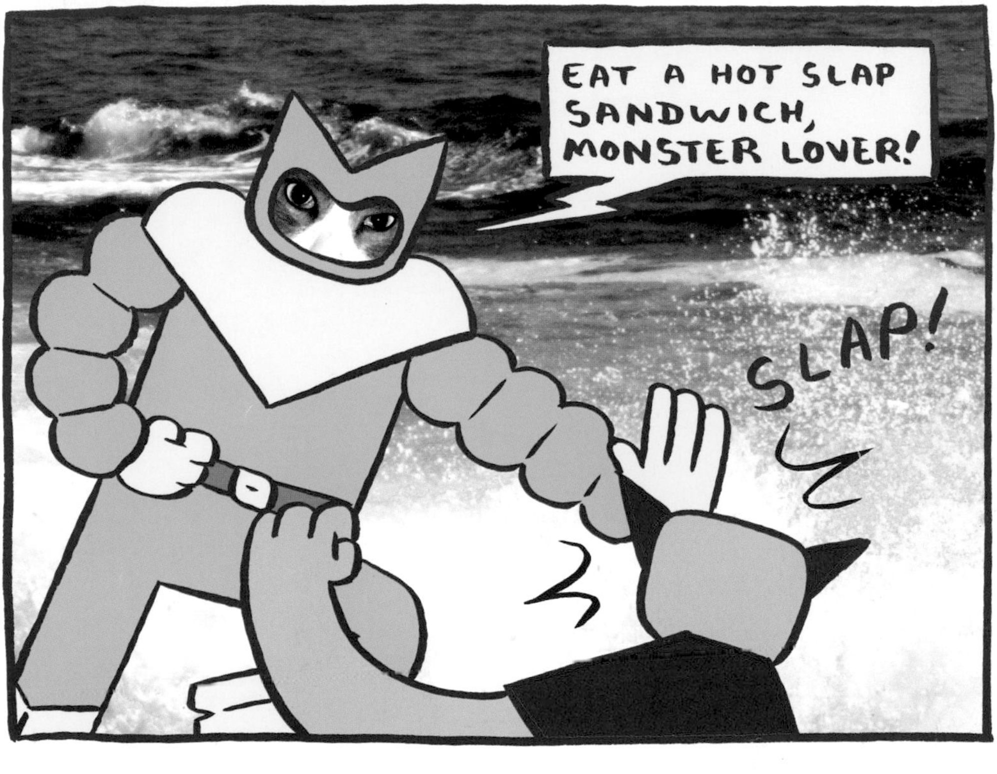
EAT A HOT SLAP SANDWICH, MONSTER LOVER!
SLAP!

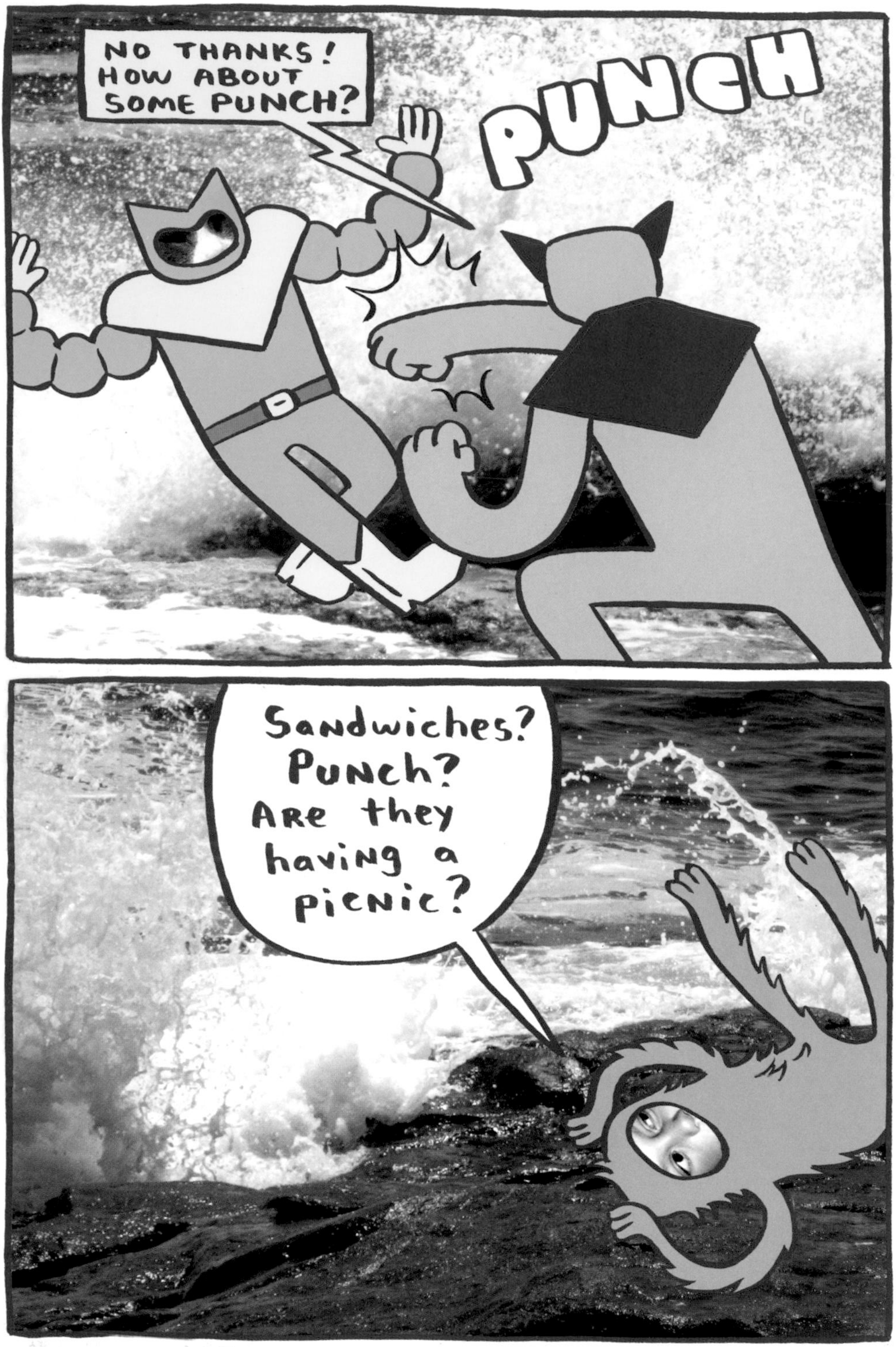
NO THANKS! HOW ABOUT SOME PUNCH?
PUNCH
Sandwiches? Punch? Are they having a picnic?

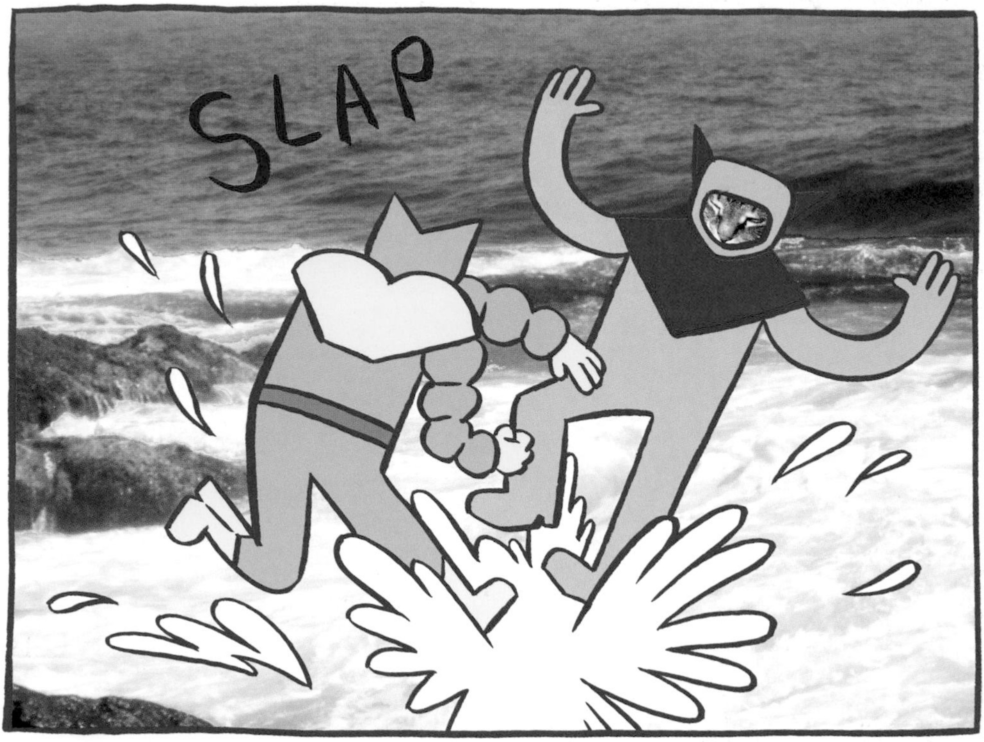
SLAP

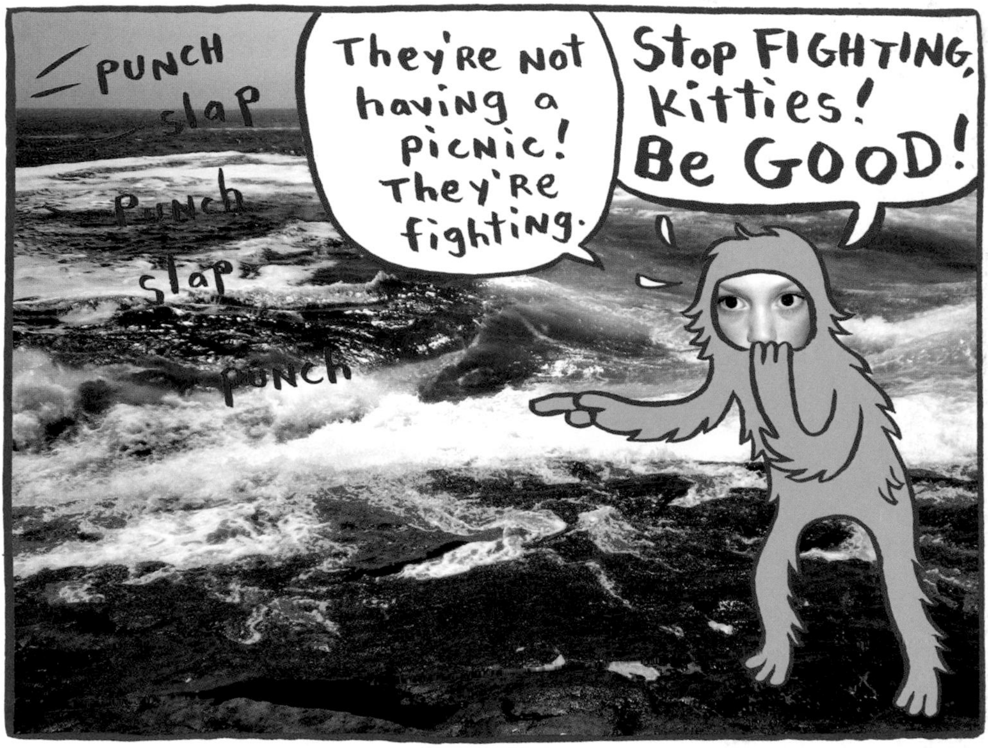
PUNCH
slap
PUNCH
slap
punch
They're not having a picnic! They're fighting.
Stop FIGHTING, kitties! Be GOOD!

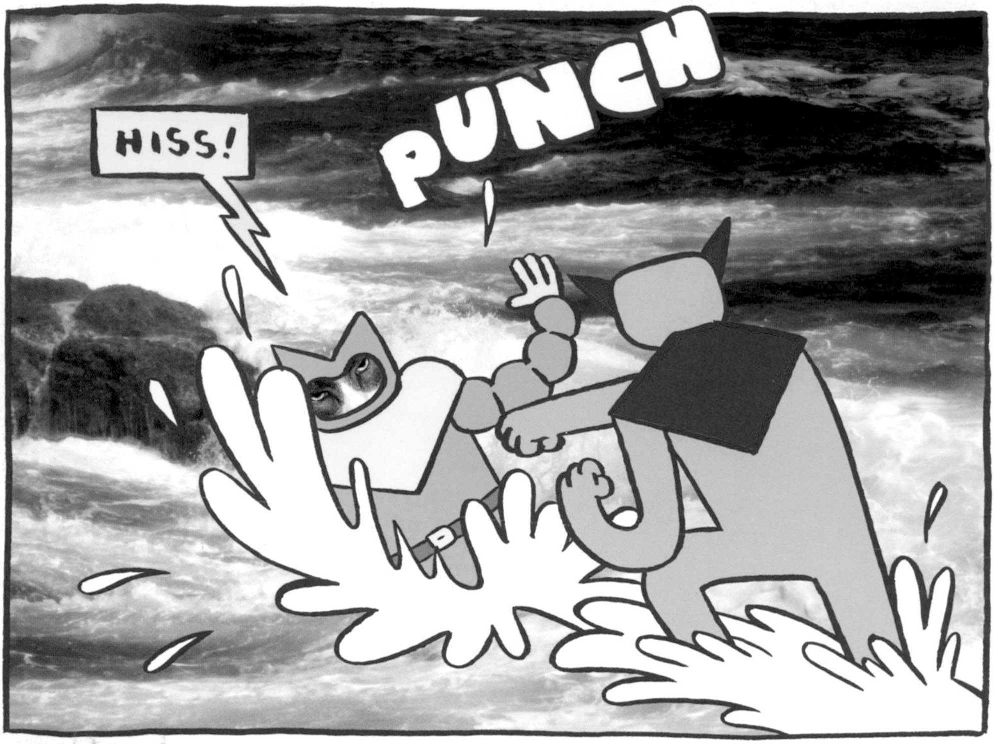
HISS!
PUNCH

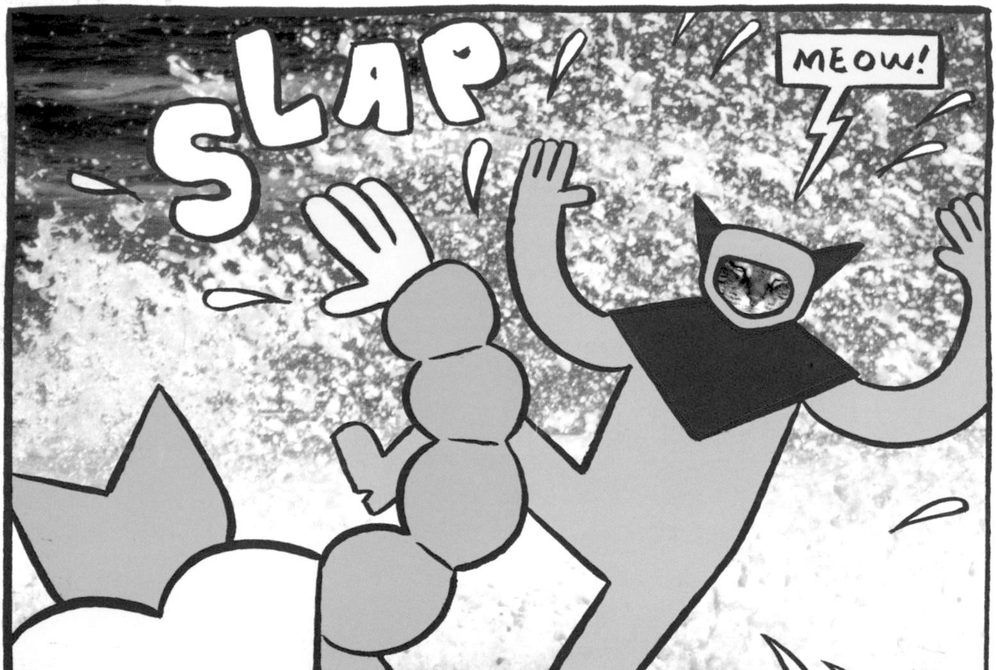
SLAP
MEOW!

SLAP
PUNCH
SLAP
Oh, if I only had my Spoony Spoon. I'd straighten them out.
But it fell into the gravy. I mean the ocean.

Oh, Spoony Spoon!
please come back to me!

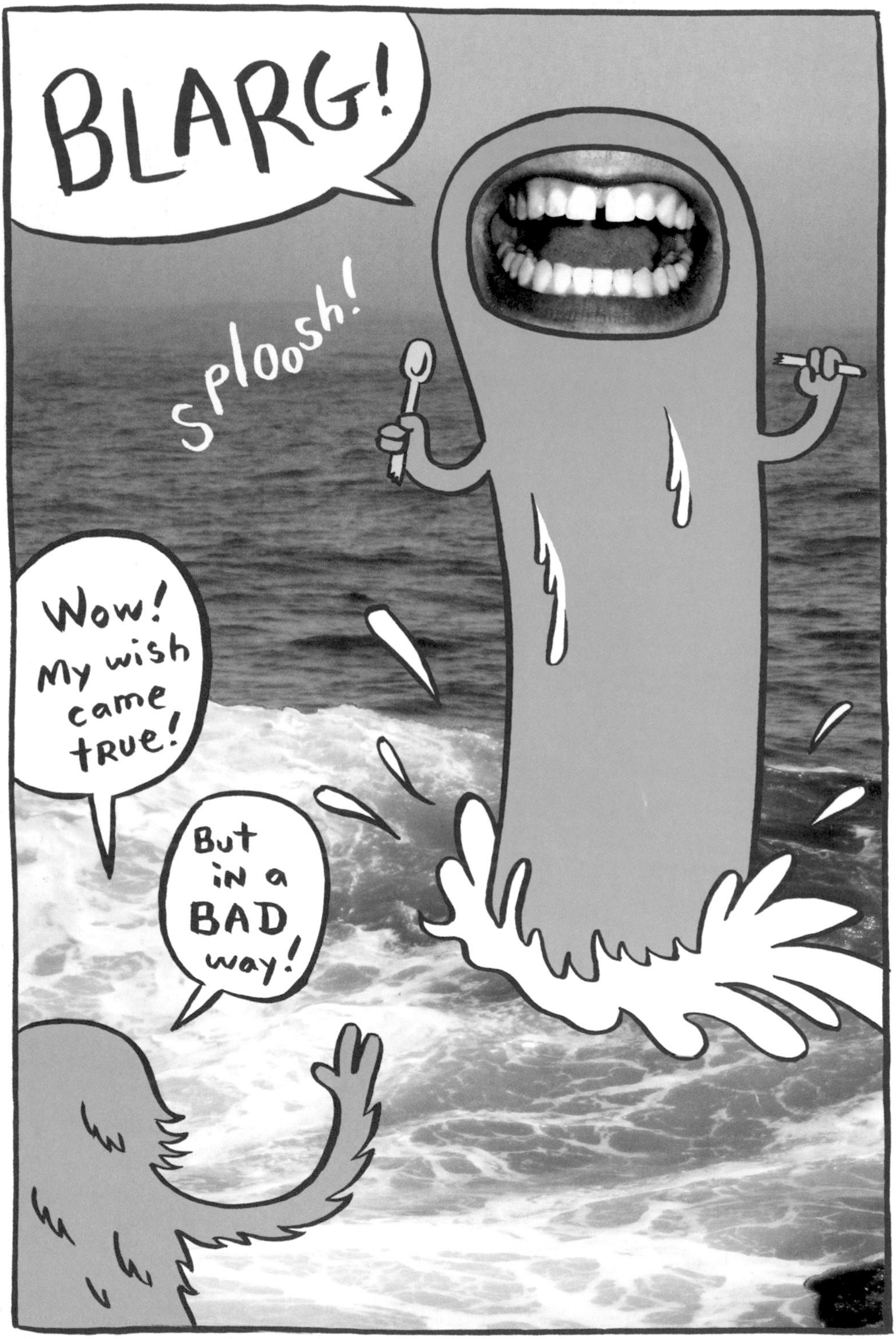
BLARG!
sploosh!
Wow! My wish came true!
But in a BAD way!

CHAPTER FIVE:

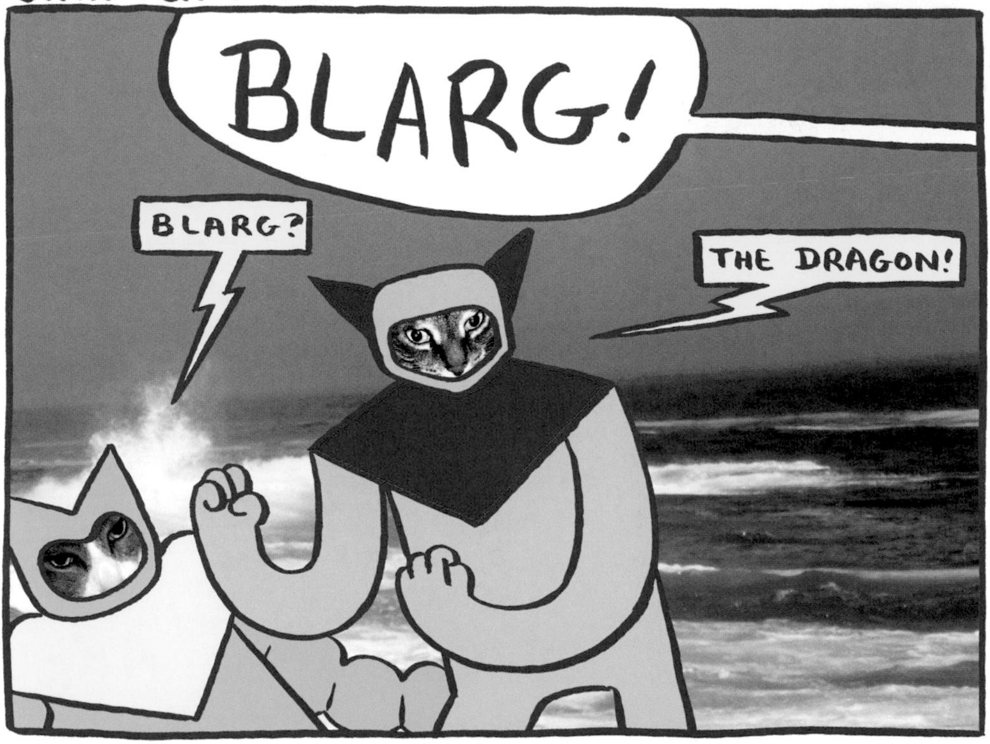
BLARG!
BLARG?
THE DRAGON!

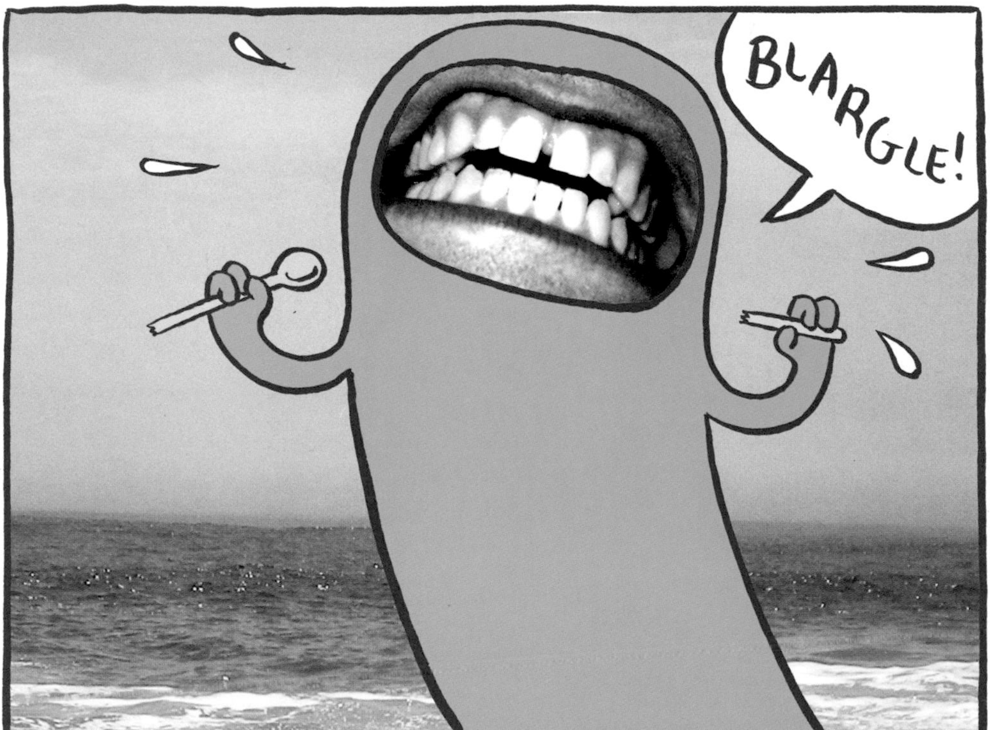
BLARGLE!

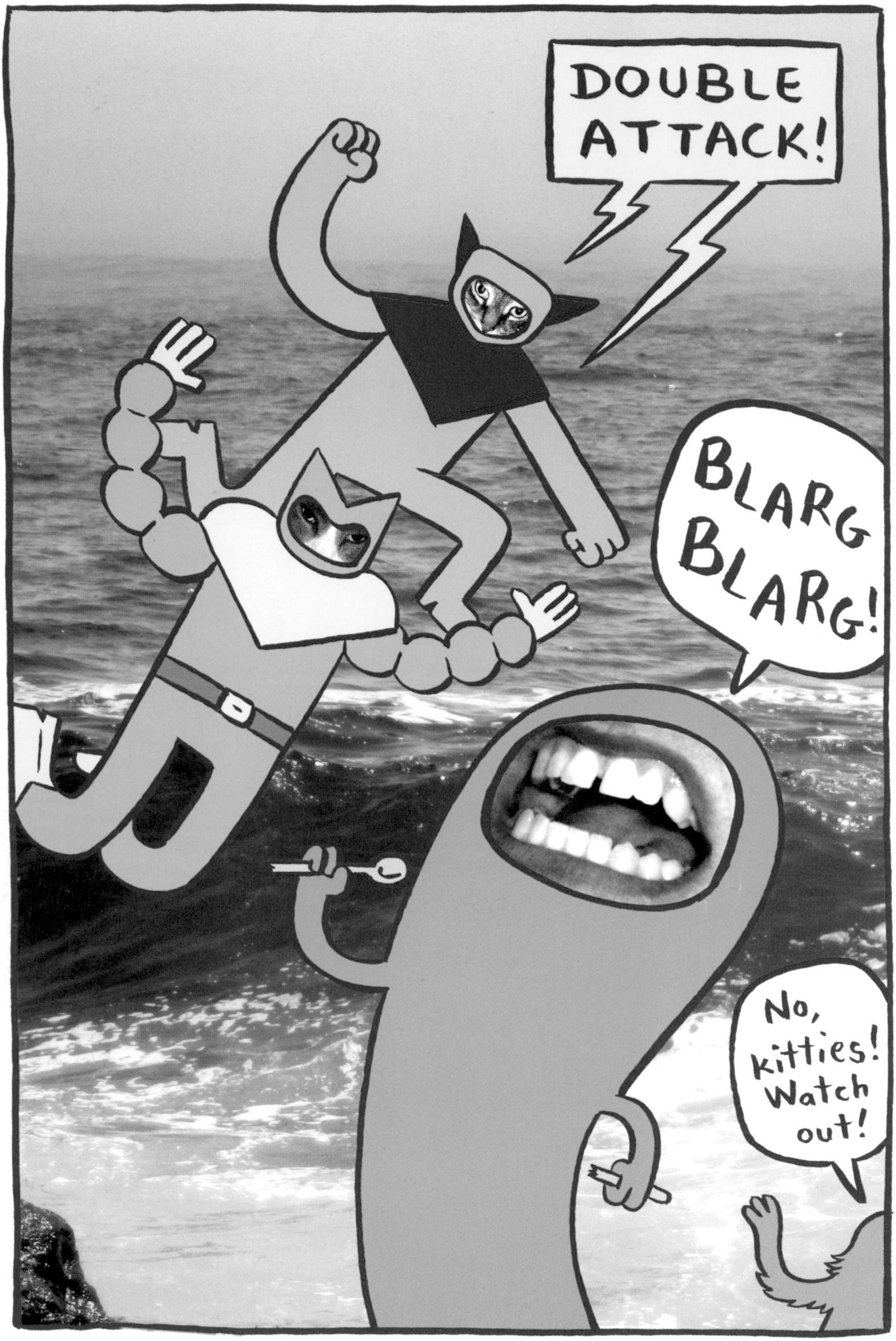
DOUBLE ATTACK!
BLARG BLARG BLARG!
No, kitties! Watch out!

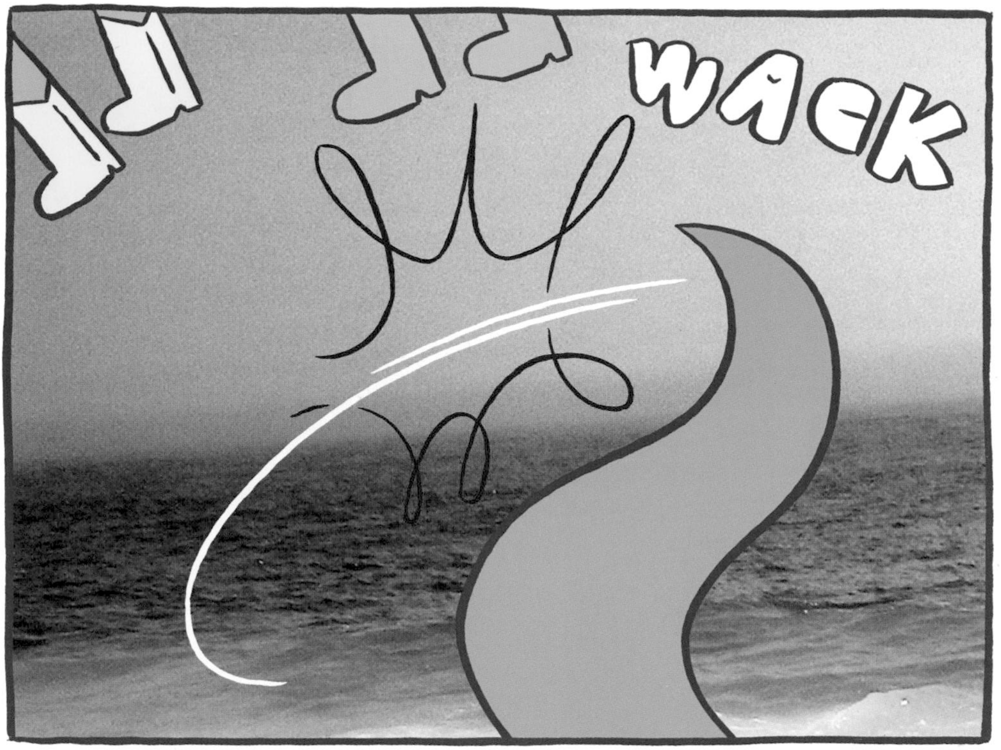
WACK

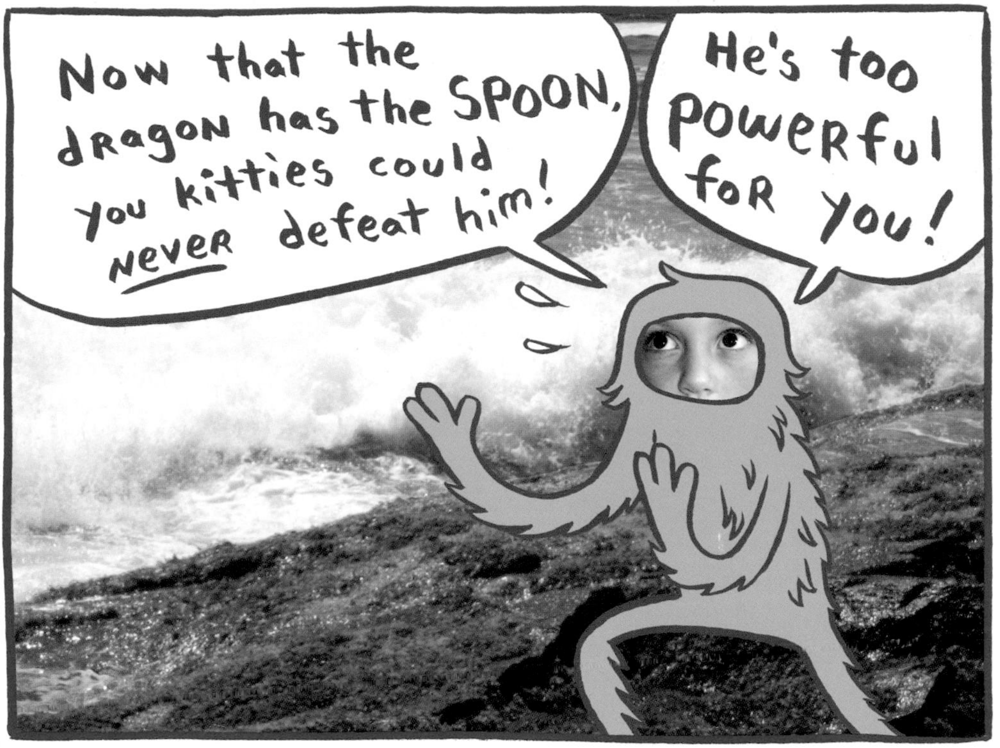
Now that the dragon has the SPOON, you kitties could NEVER defeat him!
He's too powerful for you!

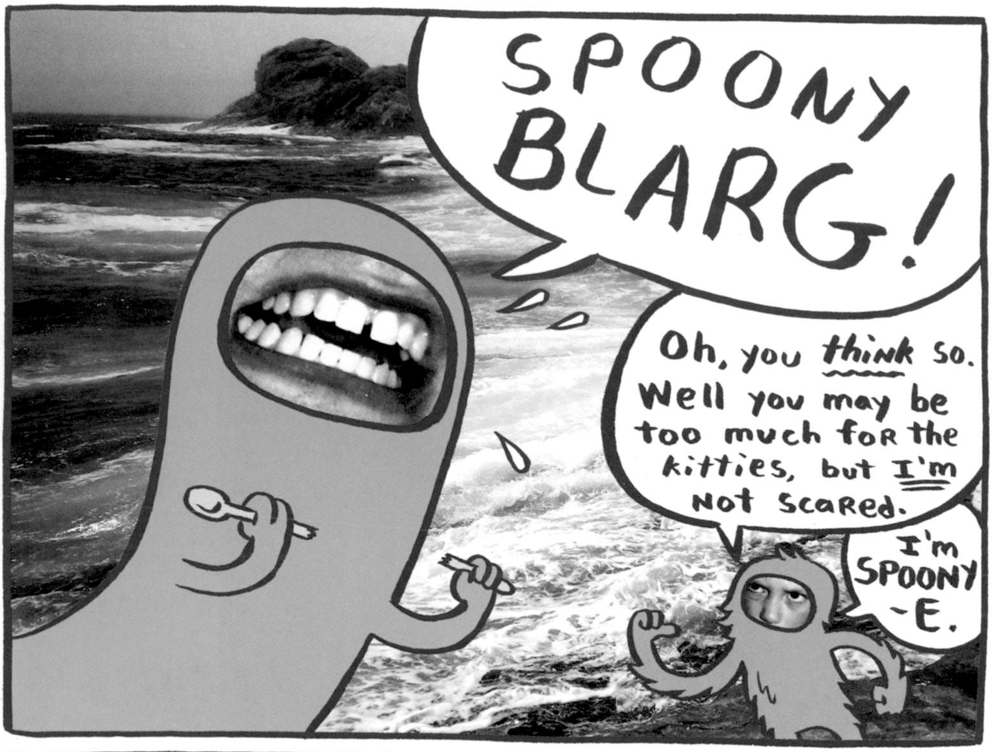
SPOONY BLARG!
Oh, you think so. Well you may be too much for the kitties, but I'm not scared.
I'm SPOONY-E.

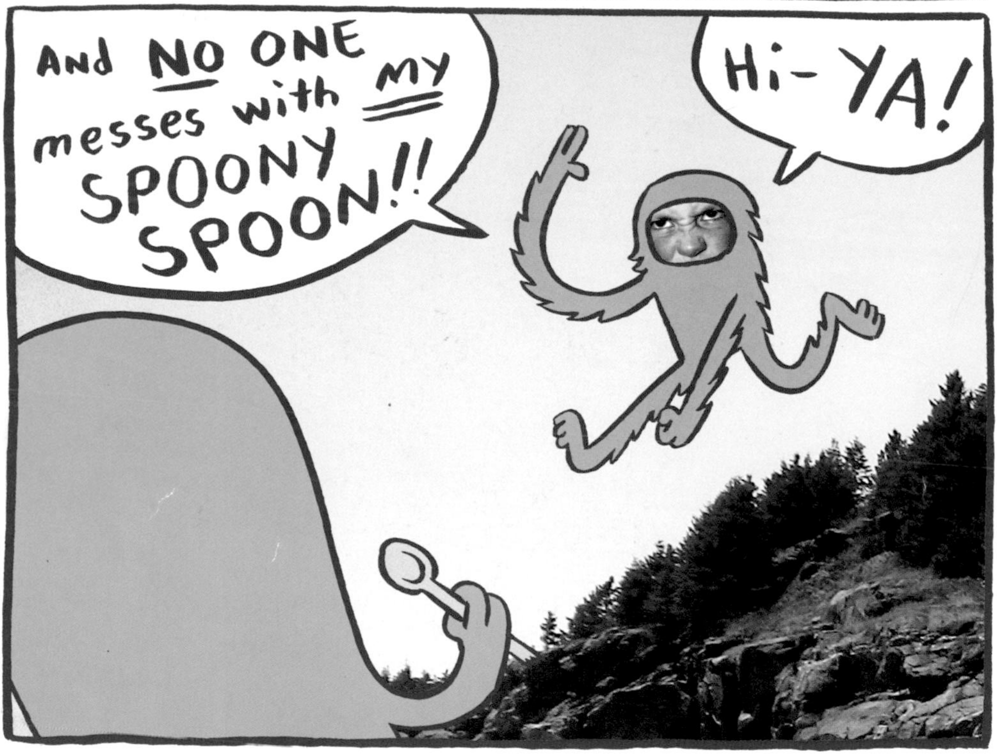
And NO ONE messes with MY SPOONY SPOON!!
Hi-YA!

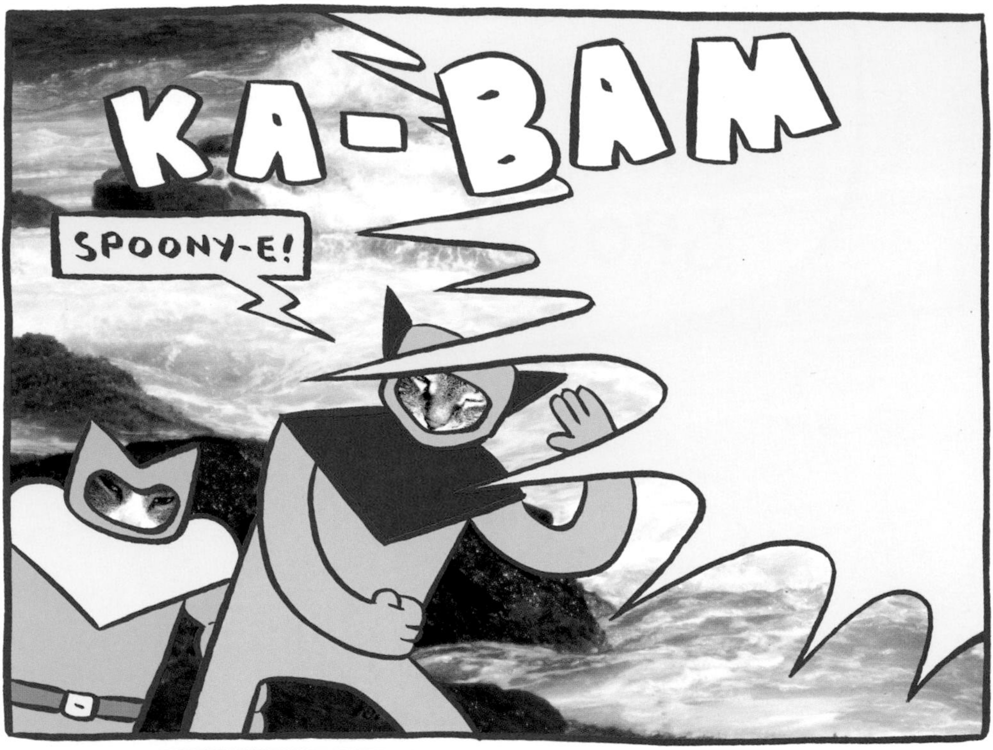
KA-BAM
SPOONY-E!

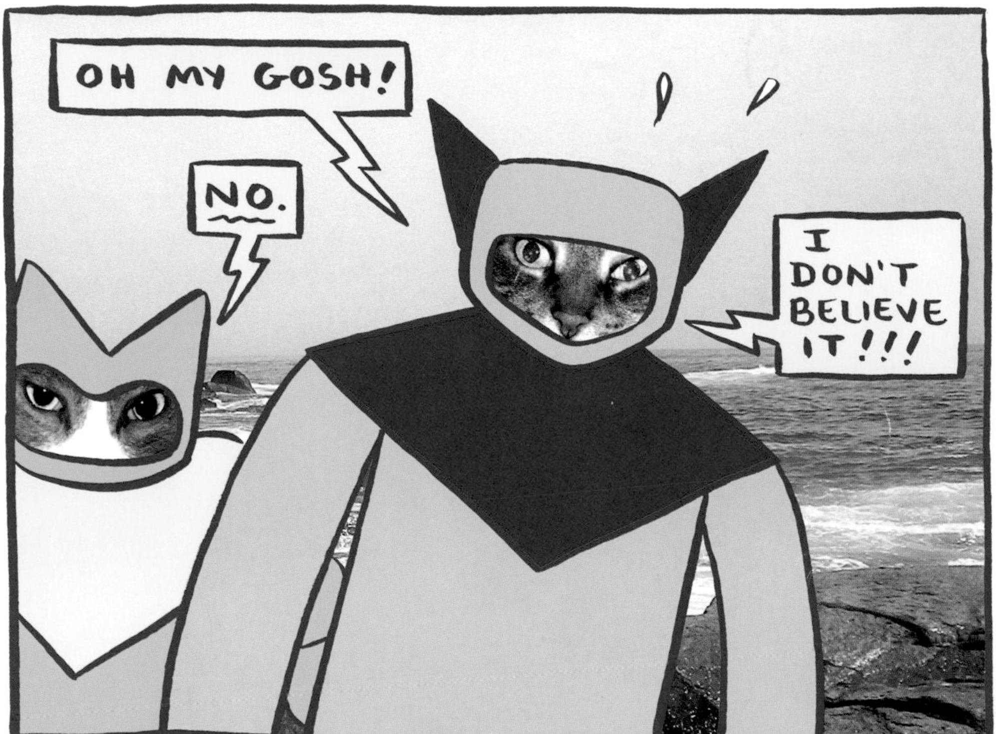
OH MY GOSH!
NO.
I DON'T BELIEVE IT!!!

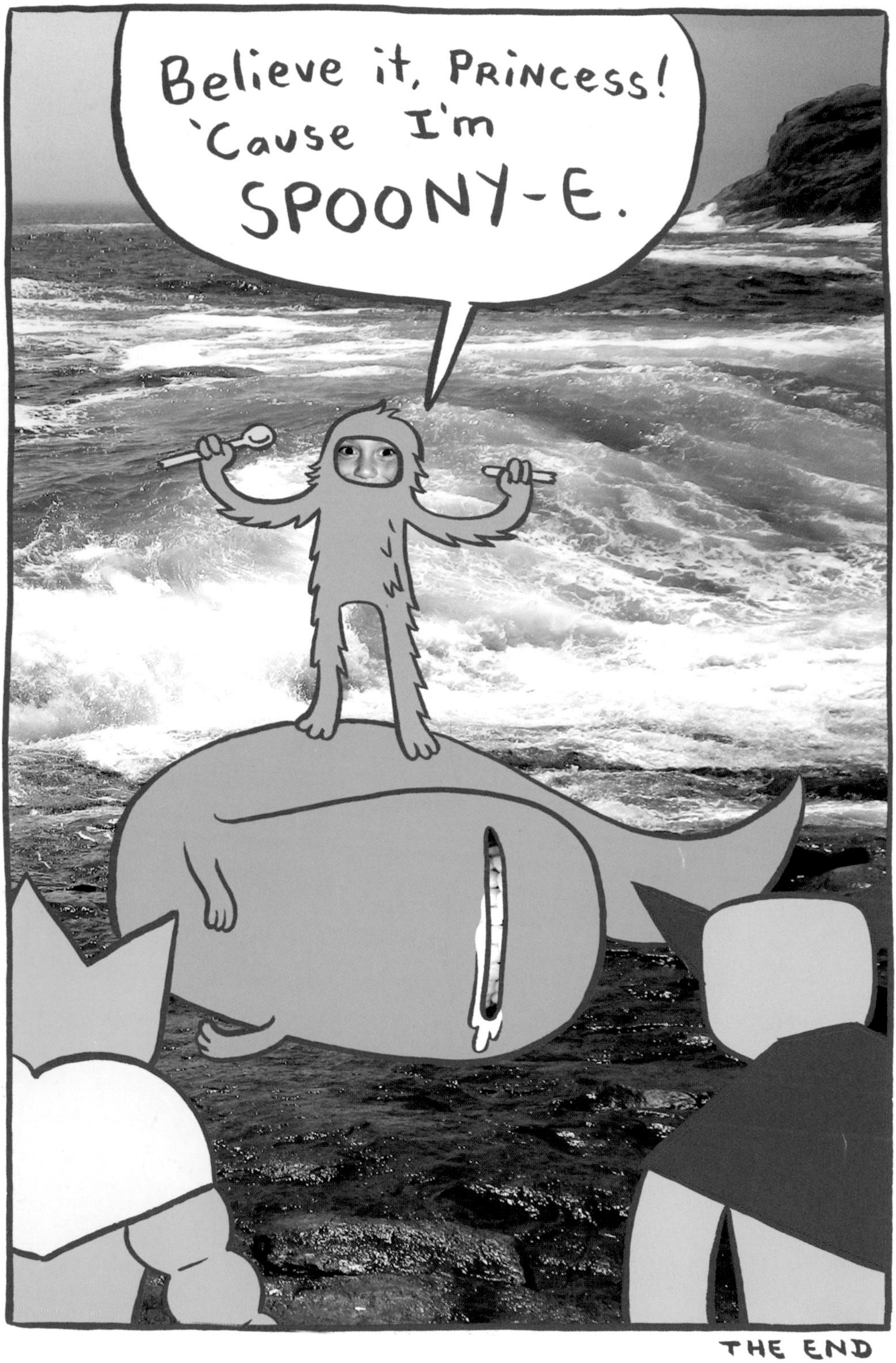
Believe it, PRINCESS! `Cause I'm SPOONY-E.

THE END

EPILOGUE:

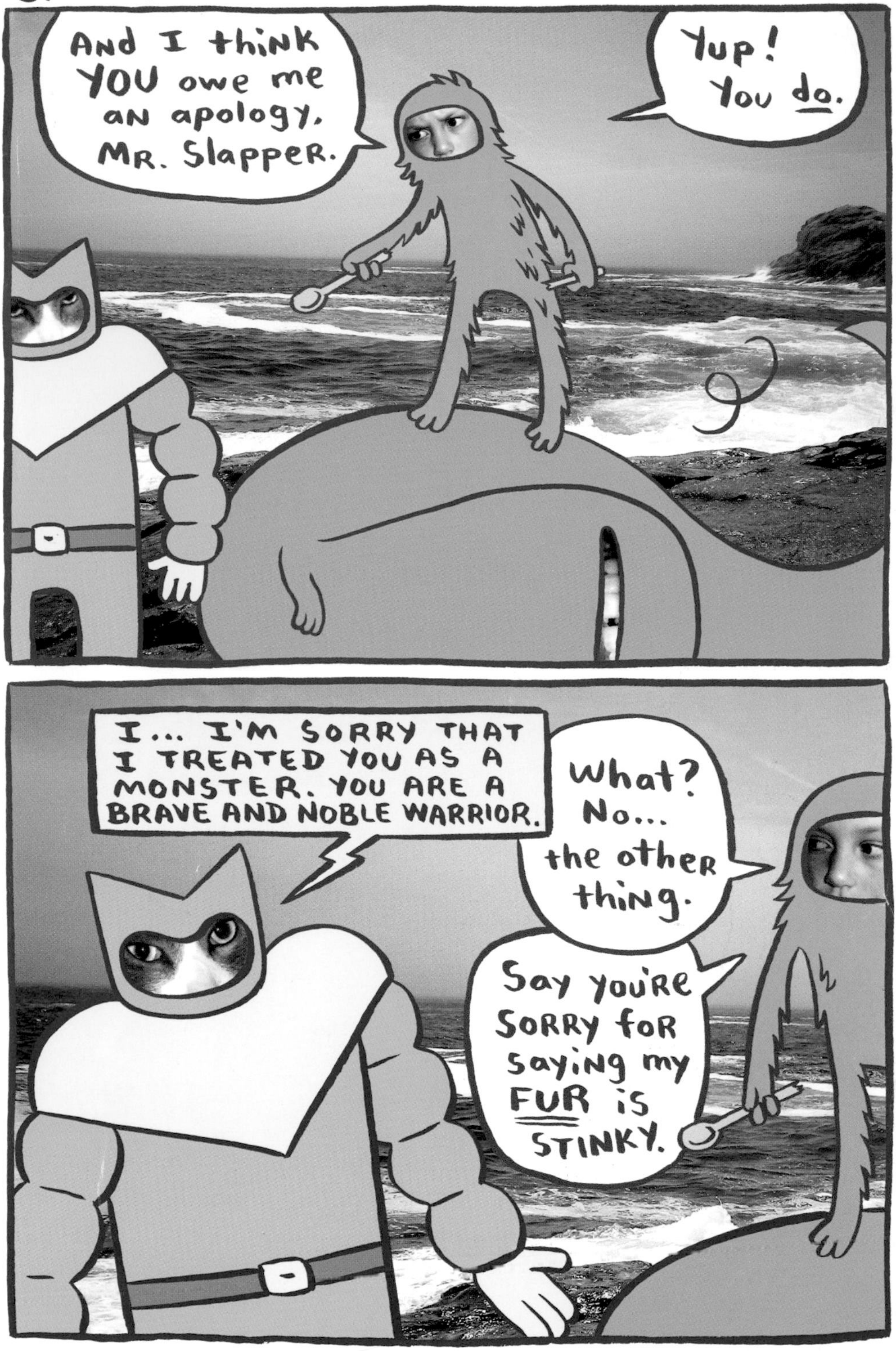
And I think YOU owe me an apology, Mr. Slapper.
Yup! You do.
I... I'M SORRY THAT I TREATED YOU AS A MONSTER. YOU ARE A BRAVE AND NOBLE WARRIOR.
What? No... the other thing.
Say you're sorry for saying my FUR is STINKY.

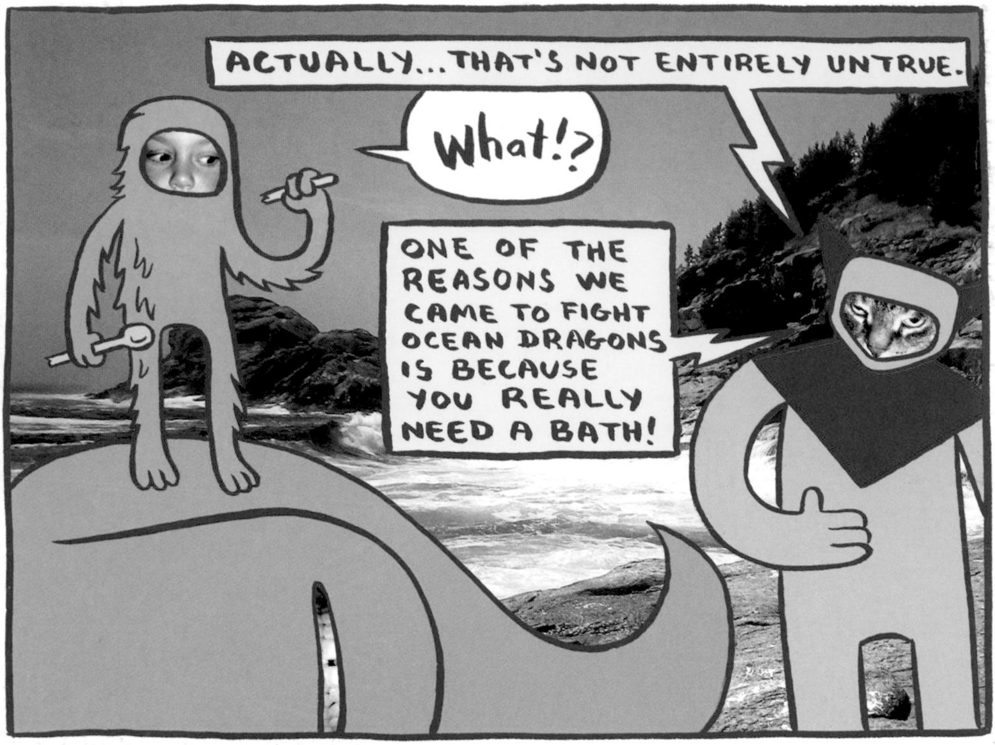
ACTUALLY... THAT'S NOT ENTIRELY UNTRUE.
What!?
ONE OF THE REASONS WE CAME TO FIGHT OCEAN DRAGONS IS BECAUSE YOU REALLY NEED A BATH!

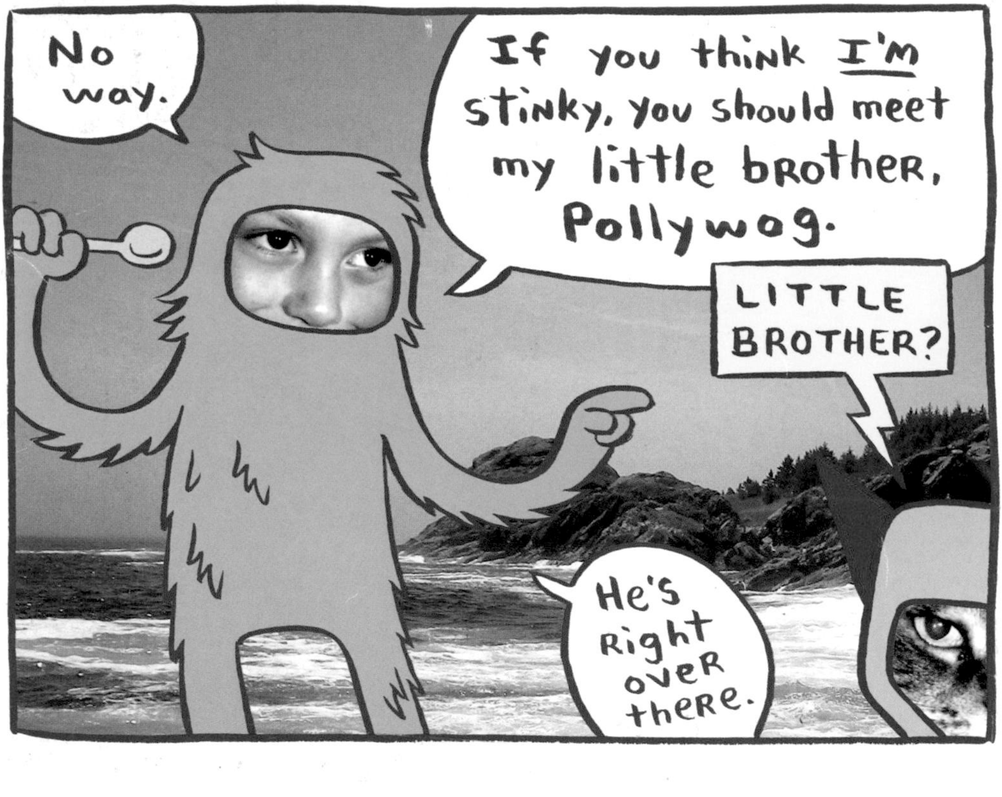
No way.
If you think I'M stinky, you should meet my little brother, Pollywog.
LITTLE BROTHER?
He's Right over there.

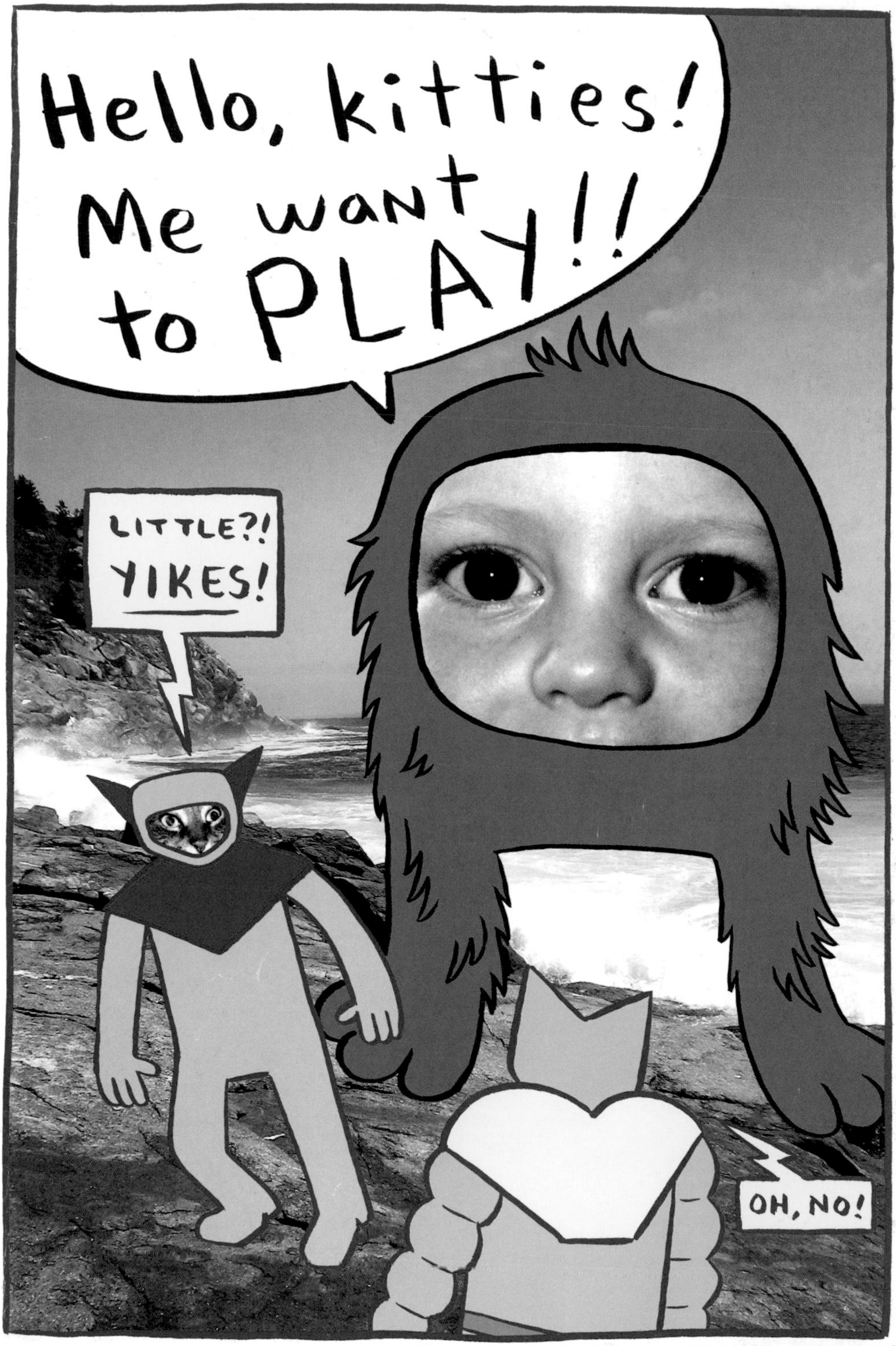
Hello, kitties! Me want to PLAY!!
LITTLE?! YIKES!
OH, NO!

BUT THAT'S ANOTHER STORY!

STARRING:

ELI KOCHALKA
AS SPOONY-E.
AGE 6

SPANDY AS THE
DRAGON PUNCHER.
AGE 16

JAMES KOCHALKA
AS THE OCEAN
DRAGON.
AGE 44

NOOKO AS THE
MONSTER SLAPPER.
AGE 1

OLIVER KOCHALKA
AS POLLYWOG.

AGE 2½